NO *Small* PARTS

ALLY BLUE

Riptide Publishing
PO Box 1537
Burnsville, NC 28714
www.riptidepublishing.com

No Small Parts

Cover art: L.C. Chase, lcchase.com/design.htm
Editors: Delphine Dryden, May Peterson
Layout: L.C. Chase, lcchase.com/design.htm

ISBN: 978-1-62649-502-9

First edition
December, 2016

Also available in ebook:
ISBN: 978-1-62649-501-2

NO
Small
PARTS

ALLY BLUE

A BLUEWATER BAY STORY

RIPTIDE
PUBLISHING

For Sarah, who invited me into the Bluewater Bay universe.
Thank you. :)

TABLE OF CONTENTS

CHAPTER ONE

"Nat. Wake up."

Nathaniel brushed a vague hand at whatever dream person was bugging him. "Go 'way."

"You're already late. You have to get up."

Wait. He knew that voice. Low, scratchy, nervous.

So. Not a dream.

Odds were he wasn't actually late, but he couldn't avoid dealing with his dad when he got insistent.

Nat forced himself upright, hauled his eyelids open, and squinted at the ancient clock radio on his bedside table. The skull sticker he'd stuck on the table's peeling paint in high school glared back at him with its one remaining eye socket. "Christ, Dad. It's only seven thirty in the morning."

"You said you had to be on set at *six* thirty. You're an hour late already." Jerome Horn nudged Nat's chest with a thin, trembling finger. "They're going to fire you, and *then* where will we be?"

"I have to be there at 6:30 *p.m.* It's a night shoot. Like last night. Remember? I didn't get home till three in the morning? Which was four and a half hours ago?"

Realization dawned on his father's face, followed by a flood of guilt, and Nat wished he'd kept his mouth shut. He knew his dad had a hard time remembering his *Wolf's Landing* shooting schedule, in spite of the paper stuck on the rust-spotted fridge with *Wolf's Landing* magnets. Hell, Nat had trouble himself sometimes. He'd worked nights before. But his part-time werewolf gig on Bluewater Bay's wildly popular TV series had him going from indoor daytime set shoots to midnight forest shoots and back again. It was crazy and sometimes exhausting.

Worth it, he thought, picturing the barely controlled chaos that somehow created weekly magic.

The money was nothing to sneeze at either, considering the sporadic nature of the work and how little other income he had.

Nat's father edged toward the door. "Sorry. You go on back to sleep."

God, he wanted to, but . . . "What're you gonna do?"

"Me? Oh, don't worry about your old dad. I'll keep myself occupied."

Last time his dad said that, Nat had found him curled up in agony on the hall floor, where he'd fallen after getting a bad muscle spasm while trying to fix the broken hinge on his bedroom door. No way was Nat letting that happen again.

"Naw, I think I'm gonna get up and make breakfast." Nat kicked the covers aside, stood, and stretched. "You want some scrambled eggs?"

"I'm not really hungry."

"C'mon, Dad. You know you can't take your Flexeril on an empty stomach." Nat glanced sideways at his father as they left the bedroom and started across the squeaky old floor to the kitchen. Food or no food didn't really matter with Flexeril, but sometimes this was the only way Nat could get his dad to eat. The logging accident four years ago had robbed him of his appetite as well as his health. "I can make pancakes if you'd rather have that."

A rare spark of interest lit the elder Horn's eyes. "I do love pancakes."

"I know." Nat rubbed a hand between his father's shoulder blades. Gently, so the touch wouldn't trigger any of the muscle spasms that had plagued him since the accident. "Go lie down on the couch. I'll bring you your pancakes on the TV tray, okay?"

"All right." His dad smiled. "Thanks, son."

"Sure."

His father shuffled off to the sagging old sofa, and Nat went to the kitchen to gather supplies for a pancake breakfast. He got out the eggs, milk, and pancake mix, found a bowl in the top cabinet, then wrestled the pancake turner out of the drawer that wouldn't ever stay on track. Jesus, this kitchen was falling apart. Probably because it was older than him and his dad put together. Nothing worked anymore.

"Nat?"

"Hmm?"

"You heard from Abby lately?"

He planted both palms on the counter and clenched his teeth until the usual surge of anger passed. He'd never blamed his sister for running off with her boyfriend all those years ago. She and their dad had never gotten along, mostly because he'd always subtly discouraged her dreams. Implied that her place was here in Bluewater Bay looking after her family, not out in the world making something of herself. Nat had been thirteen when she left, old enough that he'd understood her side of things. Old enough that he'd also understood all the ways their father treated him differently than he treated Abby.

Then the accident had happened, and she hadn't come back. Not even for a little while, to help him get situated. She'd sent money, which he'd needed and resented. But she'd left Nat to deal with it. She'd gone on with her awesome life in New York, while Nat had left behind his tiny Port Angeles apartment with the gorgeous mountain view and the lawn-maintenance job he'd enjoyed to move back home and become his father's caretaker.

No, he didn't blame Abby for leaving. But he'd never forgiven her for not coming back.

Sometimes she'd email him. Occasionally he'd email her back. But they would never be as close as they'd been as children. Her staying away lay between them like the Grand Canyon.

"Nat?"

He closed his eyes. Breathed deep. Blew it out and opened his eyes again. "I got an email the other day, yeah. She's expanding the shop, and Colin got a showing at some super popular gallery."

His father let out a gravelly laugh. "Well, I'm glad for 'em, though I don't understand why people buy that modern art. The way I see it, if it's something *I* could've painted, it ain't art, you know?"

Nat kept his own opinions behind his teeth. He didn't want to think about Colin and his ugly fucking paintings, or how happy he and Abby were and how great their life was. The bitterness might drown him.

Turning his thoughts to *Wolf's Landing* instead, he took the crappy store-brand coffee out of the cabinet and focused on brewing a pot.

"Cut! Perfect." The director, Anna, flashed her wide grin around at the *Wolf's Landing* cast and crew. "All right, people, that's a wrap. Great job, everybody."

The silence surrounding the take broke into talk and laughter as the actors drifted toward the makeup trailers in the parking area down the road, while the crew started breaking down the set. They'd been out in the forest for more than six hours, shooting the last bit of a particularly dramatic episode, and it was now nearly one in the morning. Everybody was anxious to put another late Friday shoot behind them and get some sleep.

Everyone but Nat. Tired as he was, he didn't want to leave. Not yet.

He loved the woods. Loved the quiet of it, the wet-earth smell of it, the way the branches always dripped water down the back of his neck even if it hadn't rained lately. Night was the best time to be out here, especially when the moon was full and the sky was clear. Ever since he was a kid, he'd loved stretching out in the damp mulch under the trees and gazing up at the stars glittering between the leaves.

Of course, these days he had a brighter star to watch.

He ducked his head and pretended to be busy on his phone when Solari Praveen hurried by, her stride quick and determined like it always was. She was so close he caught a whiff of her perfume as she passed. Something softly spicy, like vanilla and cloves. He lifted his gaze to watch her go up to Anna and start talking, gesturing with her hands. She was a tiny thing, probably a foot shorter than him, everything about her small and delicate, yet she projected power and fierceness with every movement. Her thick black hair flowed and shimmered in the moonlight, the ends brushing the curve of her waist. Simply looking at her made his heart pound so hard it hurt.

He stood there, knees shaking and pulse thumping at the base of his throat, trying to get his shit together before she could turn around and spot him. Sure, he wanted her to notice him, only he didn't. At least, not like this, all sweaty and nervous and tongue-tied. If she so much as glanced his way right now, he'd probably faint or piss his pants. And wouldn't *that* make a great impression?

At least she's a woman. You don't have to be so careful if you get together.

He stifled a snicker. Yeah, like that was gonna happen.

"Hey, Horn Dog."

Startled, Nat spun around too fast and almost tripped. He glared at his friend Suzanne, who laughed. "It's not funny, Suz."

"It kind of is." She peered over his shoulder, hands in her jeans pockets. "You still crushing on Stargirl?"

That was none of her damn business, so he didn't answer. "Don't call me that. I hate it."

Her smile twisted, turning sharp. "I'll trade you. Don't call me Fag Hag, I won't call you Horn Dog."

He wrinkled his nose. Or at least, tried to. The werewolf prosthetics got in the way. "Fine. But if you don't want me to call you that, you have *got* to stop trying to set me up with guys."

She tilted her head sideways, making her look like a puppy on account of her two high-set ponytails. "Huh? But I did so *good* last time. You and Lem dated for, like, six months. That's a record for you."

It was. And for a while, it had been great. Then Lem had started getting more serious than Nat was comfortable with. When he'd said so, Lem had called him emotionally unavailable, Nat had countered with "Fuck you," and their sort-of relationship had slammed head-on into the breakup wall.

Of course, his father's constant nagging at Nat to *Stop with the gay stuff, why can't you find a woman since you ain't particular,* hadn't helped. Might have even given the relationship car a nudge downhill. But Nat didn't blame his dad. Especially since cutting ties with Lem had been more of a relief than a heartbreak.

Not that he was telling Suz any of that.

He cast a cautious glance around at the dwindling crowd. Anna caught his eye for a brief second and raised her eyebrows at him, as if to ask if all was well. He waved and smiled, then edged closer to Suz and dropped his voice. "I don't want everyone here to know I'm bi, that's all."

Suz narrowed her eyes. "Since when have you been in the closet?"

"I'm not. I just don't want everybody *knowing*. You know?"

"Uh-huh. You like your privacy. I get it."

They'd been friends long enough that he knew she did, in spite of her teasing tone. "And I hate 'Horn Dog' even more now than I did in high school, so, c'mon. Please?"

"Yeah, okay." She held out her hand. "Shake."

He shook. They smiled at each other, and he felt better.

He plopped down onto a mossy tree trunk. Suz settled herself beside him. They sat and watched in silence as the crew hauled away the lights, the generators, the cameras, and the bits of set that took the forest from its usual verdant beauty into something otherworldly. Solari walked beside Anna, keeping pace with the taller woman's longer stride and talking nonstop, her hands in constant motion.

Solari's assistant sidled up to her and handed her a large mug of something that sent steam curling into the chilly night air. He caught Nat's eye and smiled. Nat nodded back, feeling like he'd been spotlighted. Why did the guy smile at him?

Suz grinned. "Are you flirting?"

"What? No. Being friendly, is all. I mean, he smiled at me, so…" He watched the assistant—what the hell was the guy's name, anyway?—accept Solari's distracted thanks with a nod, then hurry away again to do whatever assistants to TV stars did all day. He glanced Nat's way again. Favored him with another smile. He had dimples. "He's cute, though."

Suz cut him a sly look. "He's gay, you know."

Jesus Christ. Nat resisted the urge to hide his face in his hands. "So?"

"So, you should talk to him."

He almost laughed. Cute Assistant Guy might be a mere flunky, but he was still so far out of Nat's league it was stupid. "Yeah, no. I don't think so."

"Suit yourself." Suz took his hand and squeezed. "So. When're you gonna make your move?"

"What'd I just say?"

"On *Solari*, moron."

"Oh." The very idea gave him hives. "Never. I'll admire from afar until I get over it."

Suz snorted. "Way to go there, champ."

"Shut up." He watched, heart aching, as the woman he longed for said goodnight to Anna with a wave and a dazzling smile, then headed for the trailers in the parking area, where taking off *her* makeup wouldn't involve anything more than some cold cream. "She'd laugh in my face."

"No, she wouldn't."

Impossible hope rose in Nat's heart, threaded through with pure terror. He stomped it down, because, come on. "You can't tell me she'd actually go out with me."

"How the hell do I know? But she's way too nice to *laugh* at you."

"Wait, you know her?" There went that crazy, scary hope again. He told himself to stop it.

Suz shook her head. "Naw, not really. I've met her, though, when I got sent over to help out with makeup to the stars that one time. She was super nice to me. And everybody else always says she's really cool and down-to-earth."

He was still turning that over in his head, wondering what to do with it, when Anna walked over, hands in her jacket pockets. "Hi, Nat. Suz."

They both scrambled to their feet. "Hi, Anna." Nat still felt weird calling the director by her first name, but she insisted, and everyone else did it, so he did too. "What's up?"

"I'd like to talk to you about something, Nat." Anna smiled at Suz. "Could you excuse us for a minute?"

Suz nodded. "Sure. I should be getting to the makeup trailer, anyway. See you in a few, Nat."

"Yeah, see you."

She jogged off, casting him a wide-eyed glance over her shoulder.

He swallowed, his throat dry from the adrenaline rush. "So, Anna. What did you need to talk about?" Fear had his pulse thumping way too fast. He'd never get rich at this job, but right now it was the main reason he managed to keep food on the table. His part-time job with his uncle's charter boat didn't pay much. If Anna fired him, he didn't know what he was going to do.

Sympathy softened her expression. "Don't worry, it's not anything bad."

Heat rushed into Nat's cheeks. Thank God for the wolf face hiding his blush. Stupid pale skin. "Um. Okay. Good."

Her eyes took on the sharp glint that reminded him why she was a well-respected director. "Actually, I was wondering if you'd consider tackling a higher profile role. Maybe even a speaking part."

Okay, he hadn't expected that. "What?"

"I'm not talking about a full-time, major role here. I want to be clear on that." She shifted her weight from one foot to the other, still watching his face with uncomfortable intensity. "But as a physical actor, you're a natural. I'd like to bring you more to the front, give you a line here and there, and see what you can do. If you're willing, that is."

He managed to suppress the urge to let out a victory whoop, but it was a near thing. "I'd love that. Thank you." Overcome with gratitude—and, honestly, excitement—he grasped her hand and shook it. "I won't let you down, Anna. Thank you so much for this opportunity. Seriously."

"Hey, you wouldn't be getting it if I didn't think you could do it." She pressed his hand between both of hers for a moment, then let go. Her smile held a tilt that said she had an idea of how much the extra money would mean to him. She pulled her jacket tighter around her as a cool, damp breeze flowed through the trees. "You and I can get together with the legal people and the union reps and hammer out your new contract details in the next few days, if that works for you."

Terror and anticipation slammed into Nat's gut. God this was a *speaking* role. Like, actually *saying words on TV*. Yeah, it was exciting. But now that it was an actual reality, the possibility of failure loomed like the childhood closet monster. What if he couldn't do it? What if he fucked up so bad they kicked him off the show? What if, what if, what if?

Stop it. You can do this. At least, you have to try.

He swallowed hard. "That'll be fine."

She smiled. "Great. I'll have my assistant give you a call. See you, Nat."

"Yeah. See you." He waved at her as she walked away. "Thanks again."

He stood there for a second, soaking up the happiness of the moment. Deliberately focusing on the good to drown out the nagging voice whispering, *What if you fail?* Maybe now he could save enough to buy a car he wouldn't need to fix every other day. Hell, maybe this would lead to a steadier job. Something he could count on for daily work. Then he and his dad could get a new place, he could hire someone to look after his dad while he was working, he could have a *life*, finally...

Someone's nearby laughter jolted him out of his thoughts. He shook his head. Good Lord, what was wrong with him? One mention of him *maybe* getting more screen time and he was already spending the money he didn't have yet. Inventing a life where he got to choose his own path rather than following the moldy breadcrumbs laid out for him. Like *that* was ever going to happen.

You're a daydreamer, son, said his dad's voice in his head. *Your mom always said so.*

Of course, his mother had always said if you lost your dreams, you lost yourself. But his dad never seemed to remember that part of her. He never seemed to remember *any* parts of her that meant he didn't get to passive-aggressively cut Nat down.

Oh well. Maybe a new car and house were pie-in-the-sky, but if the more visible role worked out, it really would mean more money. Possibly a *lot* more money. Which Nat definitely needed.

Shoving his hands in his jeans pockets, he strode off down the dirt road toward the makeup trailers.

When he finally got home at four fifteen in the morning, a sharp burning smell greeted him. Black smoke trickled from the kitchen doorway.

Shit.

Throwing his keys on the little table beside the door, he ran for the kitchen. A pan sat smoking on the stove, something unidentifiable charred in black lumps on the bottom. He covered his mouth and nose with his shirt, grabbed the pan, dropped it in the sink, and turned off the burner. "Dad? Where are you?" He flung open the window over the sink, crossed the sagging floor, and opened the door to the tiny backyard. Damn it, he needed to put in a smoke detector.

"Mmf." The sofa springs squealed, and his father's tousled head peered over the back of the couch. "Oh, Nat. You're home. I made dinner."

Relief and fury played tug-of-war in Nat's gut. "You nearly burned the house down. You could've *died*." He flipped the switch for the overhead fan. The old motor ground to life, and the smoke began to swirl outside. He glared at his father, heart hammering and the sour taste of fear lingering on the back of his tongue. "What the hell were you thinking? How many times have I told you not to use the stove when you're on your meds?"

His father peered at him with a remorse Nat had long ago learned not to trust. "I'm sorry. I thought I'd turned off the stove before I took my Vicodin, honest. And I wouldn't have taken it at all, but you know how my back gets when it's damp like this, then you were *so* late getting home, and I just . . . fell asleep."

"Uh-huh." Nat glanced around. The three empty beer cans weren't enough to explain the slur in his dad's voice. Not after his heavier and heavier drinking lately—both on the sly and not so much—along with increasing doses of painkillers and muscle relaxers. Christ. If he could figure out which of his dad's old drinking buddies kept supplying him with beer, Nat would have them arrested. No matter how many cans Nat poured out, more kept popping up. "How many pills did you take?"

"Only two. I swear." His dad's eyelids drifted down, settled there for a heartbeat, then rose like they weighed ten pounds each. His forehead creased, his mouth twisting in a pained rictus Nat had seen all too often. "Don't look at me like that. You don't know what it's like."

Nat turned away. The fact was, he really didn't know what it was like. He knew how his father had writhed in agony on a hospital stretcher when he was first injured. He knew he'd watched the man who'd been so physically strong all his life dwindle to a thin, stooped shadow of himself since that accident. He knew he'd seen the spark of life and hope go out of his father's eyes, replaced by the fever of addiction.

He knew his father was in constant pain—both physical and mental. But, no, he didn't know what it was like.

Worse, he had no idea how to fix it.

For a single, searing second, Nat stood there staring at the charred mess in the sink and fighting the overwhelming urge to run. To bolt out the open door and keep going until he dropped. To never look back.

But he couldn't do that, and not only because he refused to be the sort of man who abandoned his responsibilities. His father hadn't always been the shell of a person he was now. He'd been a loving, caring, attentive dad. And he'd worked hard to make sure Nat and his sister had had everything they needed after their mother died. Nat had only been seven when he'd lost his mother to cancer, but he still remembered her face, and the sound of her laugh. And he remembered his father holding him tight while he cried for his mother, telling him everything would be all right. That Dad would look after him.

Jerome Horn wasn't a perfect man, or a perfect father. But he'd been strong for his children when they needed him. The way Nat saw it, he owed his father the same now that their situations were reversed.

A soft snore told him the drugs in his dad's system had taken over again. With a sigh, Nat turned, pulled the old plaid blanket up over his father's bony frame, and went to scrub the burned pan.

CHAPTER TWO

W hen he got to work Monday morning, Rafael heard the argument going on inside Solari's trailer before he'd even gotten to the bottom of the steps.

Good God. He stopped below the tiny window she always left open and listened to the one-sided stream of vitriol. Solari Praveen yelling at her girlfriend over the phone wasn't exactly unusual, but it wasn't his favorite way to start the day. Especially when he'd finally worked up his nerve to ask her to speak to Anna for him.

Well. No point in putting off the inevitable. Squaring his shoulders, he climbed the steps and knocked on the trailer door. "Solari? Coffee's here."

The yelling stopped. "Come in."

He pulled the handle and shoved at the same time. The door swung inward with a squeal. *Wolf's Landing*'s latest sensation sat at the little round table in her bathrobe, her features twisted with fury and her cheeks flaming. Instead of ordering him to put the coffee on the counter like she usually did, she jumped up and took it from him. "Thanks."

Concerned, he watched her swivel on one bare foot and march back to her chair. "Everything all right?"

"Fine."

He raised his eyebrows at her. She gulped coffee, then set her cup down so hard drops of brown liquid splashed through the opening in the plastic lid. "That horrible, horrible *cow*. How *dare* she treat me like this."

"What did she do?" God, this was *so* none of his business. But Solari obviously needed to vent, and if he helped her out now, maybe she'd help him out later. Plus he really did like her. She was a nice person and he hated to see her upset.

"She said she'd leave me if I don't go public with our relationship."

Rafael shuffled from foot to foot, uncomfortable and unsure what to say.

"Well, not in those exact words," Solari continued before Rafael could come up with anything suitably supportive. "She said she was tired of being my *dirty little secret*"—those three words spoken in a whisper—"and if I was that ashamed of her, maybe we shouldn't be together at all."

Having been a closeted man's down-low lover before, Rafael couldn't disagree. On the other hand, coming out in Hollywood could be pretty awful. On the hypothetical third hand, this was absolutely, positively *not* his business. "Uh . . ."

Solari shot him a barbed look. "Oh, yes, it's all just lovely for *you*, I suppose. You're behind the scenes. You're allowed to be whoever you like. Hollywood makes a lot of pretty noises, but an out gay woman in this business is the most chained-down creature you can imagine. I cannot and *will* not sacrifice my career for anyone. Not even Gina Carrington. I'm awfully sorry if that's a problem for the rest of the world, but it's my life and I'll live it as I see fit."

"Of course you should." He wasn't about to get into the whole thorny mess that was a gay person's life in the entertainment business. Her experience was her own, and he couldn't dispute it. "I know there's nothing I can do. But if you want to talk, I'll listen."

Her features relaxed into the sweet smile that had charmed the whole country since she'd taken over the role of Alicia on the show. "I appreciate that. And I'm sorry for snapping at you. Fighting with Gina puts me in an awful mood. I hate that."

"It's okay. I totally get it." He smiled back. "I'm supposed to remind you that you're due at makeup in half an hour."

"I'll be there. Thank you." She made a shooing motion with one hand. "Now go on. I'm sure you have other things to do."

He didn't at the moment. But it didn't matter. "Sure. I'll see you later. Text me if you need anything."

She nodded, her attention already turning inward. As he left the trailer, she folded her legs beneath her in the chair and curled both hands around her coffee cup. Her expression was sad.

Rafael almost stopped, but didn't. He didn't know her well, but he'd learned enough to know when she wanted to be alone.

He pulled the door firmly shut behind him and hurried down the steps.

Not ten feet away, the tall, slender blond man who'd been blatantly staring at Solari's trailer turned away and pretended to check his phone.

Rafael studied the other man's long legs and graceful back with interest. He knew exactly two things about this person: he played one of the recurrent nonspeaking werewolves on the show, and he'd been drooling at Solari's feet practically ever since she'd arrived on set.

Well. He also knew the guy was a low-key sort of sexy. And the way his stare turned intense once he got his wolf makeup on . . . Did he even know he did that?

He was *made* for film. The camera loved him. The director in Rafael wanted to know more about this man with such a wealth of raw talent.

Acting purely on impulse, Rafael strode over and planted himself directly in front of Sexy Werewolf. "Hi. We've seen each other around set, but we haven't been formally introduced." He stuck out his hand and put on his biggest, brightest smile. "I'm Rafael Cortez, Ms. Praveen's personal assistant. Pleased to meet you."

Blondie gaped at him. "Huh?"

"I'm Rafael." He held his pose, hand out and smile in place, though he was starting to feel like an idiot. "What's your name?"

After a couple of endless, painful seconds, Sexy Werewolf *finally* shook his hand. "Nat Horn. I play a werewolf on the show." His voice was deep, slow, and soft, as if he were thinking through each word individually before he spoke. Rafael found it intriguing.

"Yeah, I've seen you act." Rafael peered up into Nat's eyes, a washed-out, almost white blue. Eyes like a husky. He'd always thought they were contacts. Apparently not. "You're a natural."

Nat's pale cheeks colored. "Um. Thanks."

"Nothing but the truth." A damp, chilly breeze flowed down the lane between trailers, and Rafael shivered. "I was about to go get some hot tea or something. You want to join me?"

Nat shrugged. "Why not? I have a few minutes before I need to be in the makeup chair."

The two of them strolled toward craft services in companionable silence. Rafael zipped his jacket all the way to his chin and wondered how Nat managed not to freeze in his thin long-sleeved T-shirt. The morning was misty and cool, like most March mornings in coastal Washington, and Rafael couldn't have survived without his fleece jacket. He'd been brought up in the southern California sunshine. This whole cold-and-damp business didn't work for him.

"So," Rafael said as they took their place in the coffee cart line. "Are you from here?"

"Yeah. Born and raised." Nat cut him a knowing look. "I don't need to ask about you."

Rafael laughed. "You got me. I'm one of those Hollywood invaders."

A crooked smile softened Nat's sharp features. "This place never had it so good."

It wasn't the first time Rafael had heard that sentiment. Seemed the town had been breathing its last before *Wolf's Landing* came along and revived it. Most of the locals loved the economic boost, if nothing else.

"It's gorgeous here. I love it." Which wasn't a lie. Hollywood held Rafael's heart, but the natural beauty of this place had knocked him sideways from the first. It still did. "And everyone's been super nice."

The sardonic arch of Nat's right eyebrow said he knew that wasn't completely true, but he didn't argue. Then it was their turn to order and the subject was dropped in favor of hot beverages.

Nat got his Americano first, because this was Washington State and coffee was king, always fresh brewed and ready to go. He went to find them a seat while Rafael waited for the girl with the green buzz cut to make him his chai tea.

When he finally got his lusciously warm cup and turned to find Nat, he was startled to see Solari standing beside Nat at the edge of the crowd. Her hand was resting on his arm, her face was tilted up toward his with that smile that had the whole world under her spell.

If Rafael didn't know better, he'd have said she was flirting.

Whether she was or not, poor Nat was clearly neck-deep in that deliciously torturous territory you fall into when your crush acknowledges your existence. His cheeks burned bright red, and he stared at Solari like she was a storybook princess magically made flesh.

Rafael watched the two of them talk, curiosity eating at him. After a couple of minutes, Solari gave Nat's arm a squeeze and hurried off toward the makeup trailer. Nat gazed after her like a starstruck tourist rather than a guy who'd shared a set with her more than once.

Rafael strolled up to Nat, cradling his tea in his palms. "What was that all about?"

Nat started, blinked, and peered at Rafael with shock stamped all over his face. "She . . . um. Nothing."

A short girl with two high ponytails leaned out the half-open door of the extras trailer. "Nat! C'mon, will you? You're gonna be late."

Nat half turned, his gaze still fixed in the middle distance. "Yeah. Coming." His eyes focused on Rafael's face. "I gotta go to makeup. I'll see you around, though, huh?"

"Yeah, for sure."

Nat grinned, gave Rafael a nod, and strode off to the makeup trailer. Rafael watched him go. No wonder Anna had wanted the guy as a werewolf. He looked like one. Hell, he even moved like one: all slinky and graceful.

Rafael's phone rang, startling him out of his thoughts. He glanced at the screen, then answered with a smile. "Hi, Mom. What's up?"

"Hi, love. I was wondering if you're going to make it home for your father's birthday party this weekend?"

"I don't think so. I have to be on set."

"Oh no. I thought you said you might be able to get a couple of days off."

"Yeah, I thought I might. But it didn't work out." Guilt needled him. "I'm sorry, Mom. I really did want to make it home."

"I know, honey. Don't worry about it. Dad knows you're thinking of him. If you could give him a call, though, he'd appreciate it."

"Sure thing. I'd love to talk to him." One of the show's other stars, Carter Samuels, leaned around the corner of the makeup trailer and mouthed, *Call me*, miming a phone to his ear with his left hand. Rafael gave him a thumbs-up. Carter flashed his megawatt smile and popped out of sight. "I have to go, Mom, I'm being paged. I'll talk to you and Dad on Sunday, okay?"

"All right, sweetheart. I love you."

"Love you too. Bye."

Rafael ended the call and gave himself a moment to brood before he called to see what Carter needed. He'd taken this job mostly for the potential to work with one of his directorial heroes, Anna Maxwell, even if he had to start—and probably stay—in the role of assistant to the stars. He didn't regret it. But his heart remained in Hollywood, with his history and his family. As much as he loved Bluewater Bay and the chance to be a part of *Wolf's Landing*, he wasn't sure he'd have had the stomach to come here if he had known how seldom he'd get to go back home.

Oh well. No point in sitting here navel-gazing. He had a long day ahead. And a long night too. He'd finished the script for *Inside*, his latest film project, and gotten some sample footage with his camcorder, but it needed editing before he could put it up on Kickstarter. And he still needed to find his lead actor, which was proving to be a serious challenge.

Pushing to his feet, he scrolled through his contacts, found Carter's number, and hit dial.

"Stay away from me, you bastard." Solari stalked forward, her eyes glittering and her small hands fisted at her side. "If you ever come near me again, I'll *kill* you."

Rafael leaned back on the sofa and grinned over his copy of the script. "Perfect. I'd hate to be Max Fuhrman right now."

Her face relaxed into a smile, though a single angry line remained stubbornly stuck between her eyes. "Thank you. I'm feeling inspired."

By the fight with Gina, no doubt. Not that he was going to say that out loud.

He stood, leaving the script on the coffee table in Solari's living room. "I think you've got that scene nailed down. Is there anything else you want to go over before I take off?" *Say no. Please say no.* He was itching to dig into edits on his sample footage before the night completely got away from him.

She shook her head. "No, you go. I need to go change anyway."

"Oh. Okay." He cast her a sidelong glance as he went to get his jacket from the coat closet beside the door. "You going out?"

"Maybe."

Maybe, my butt. "Well, have fun. See you tomorrow."

"Thanks, Rafael. Good night."

He shrugged on his jacket and opened the front door.

Nat the werewolf stood outside, his hand raised to knock.

CHAPTER THREE

N at stared, frozen. He hadn't expected to find Rafael at Solari's place when he arrived to pick her up for their date. He wasn't sure what to think.

He's gay, remember? No reason to worry. Calm down.

Easier said than done. Especially when his nerves had been screaming ever since Solari had unexpectedly asked him out that morning, and he now found himself inches from a man who was even cuter than he remembered from earlier, and smelled nice too. He licked his lips, sifting through his suddenly blank mind for appropriate words.

A weird blend of irritation and pity slid through Rafael's eyes—big, pretty, deep-brown eyes—before he smiled and held out his hand. "Hi, Nat. We meet again."

"Uh. Yeah. Hi." Nat reached out and shook Rafael's hand, more from force of habit than anything else. After a whole day of picturing the moment he'd arrive at Solari's apartment, this was so *not* how he'd imagined it. "I'm here to pick up Solari. We're . . . um . . ."

The words dried up in his throat. He dropped Rafael's hand, and they stared at one another, each taking the other's measure in silence.

Solari rescued him before it got too awkward. "Nat, hi! Please, come in."

Renewed anxiety sent his pulse galloping. He peered beyond Rafael's shoulder. Solari smiled at him from what was clearly the doorway to her bedroom, and his knees wobbled. "Hi. You look beautiful."

She laughed, and the sound was like bells. "You're so sweet, but I haven't even changed my clothes yet. Rafael, will you let him in, already?"

An angry look Nat didn't get at all hardened Rafael's soft, round features for a second. "Sure." He stepped aside with a bland smile. "You kids have a great time. Night."

Nat watched with a frown as Rafael strode out the door and shut it behind him. "Did I say something wrong?"

"Not at all. He's in a bad mood." Solari took Nat's hand and pressed his fingers. "Have a seat. I'll be ready in a moment."

Her touch stole his ability to speak. Nodding, he stumbled to the nearest chair on rubbery legs and fell into it.

This is actually happening. I'm going out on a date with Solari Praveen. Me. Nathaniel Horn.

It didn't make any sense. Part of him still half believed he'd wake up and find out the whole thing had been a dream. But in the meantime, he might as well enjoy it.

Solari emerged from the bedroom after a few minutes, wearing a long-sleeved, dark-red dress that clung to her body and swirled around her calves. He rose, dazzled and wishing he was one of those guys with the perfect words falling off his tongue all the time. He'd tell her she was a vision. A goddess. The smartest, cleverest, most stunning, most wonderful woman ever to grace the earth.

But he'd never been one of those men. He beamed his brightest smile. "I thought you looked gorgeous before, but, wow."

"Thank you." She walked up to him, her low heels clicking on the wooden floor. Smiling, she brushed her fingers over the lapels of the dark-gray suit jacket he'd bought especially for tonight. "You look very handsome yourself. I don't believe I've ever seen you in a suit. You should dress up more often."

"Thanks." He flicked imaginary lint off his sleeve and tried to pretend his face wasn't a cherry red that matched her dress. He couldn't decide if he was blushing because she'd complimented him, or because she'd evidently noticed him before today.

God, this was stupid. A twenty-six-year-old man shouldn't feel like a teenager at his first boy-girl party. He'd dated plenty of women before. Why should Solari Praveen turn him into such an idiot?

Her expression turned sympathetic. "So. Shall we go? I've made reservations at Il Trovatore."

Nat kept his mouth from falling open with an effort. Shit, an appetizer at that place probably cost more than he made in a week. "Oh. Uh, sure. Sounds great."

"Oh, it is. Anna took me there when I first started on *Wolf's Landing*, so she could discuss the character with me. The scallop fettuccini alfredo is wonderful." She led him out into the chilly night air and locked the door behind her. "Don't worry about the money. *I* asked *you* out, so I'm paying." She pointed a mock-fierce finger in his face. "And don't you dare tell me I can't because I'm a woman. I have no patience for that sort of thing. Are we clear?"

He studied her face: her sparkling eyes, the teasing curve of her full lips, the way her black hair framed her features. She was perfect. He would never tell her what she could and couldn't do, even if he were inclined. Which he wasn't.

He grinned. "Crystal clear. Lead on, milady."

Laughing, she tucked her hand in the curve of his elbow. "I like you, Nat."

"Mutual, Solari." He choked the words out past the tangle of terror and elation lodged in his throat, but if she noticed, she didn't let on.

Together, they strolled along the sidewalk to the restaurant.

Nat wasn't sure what he'd expected, but the hours that followed weren't it.

He and Solari talked and talked and talked some more at the restaurant, until their waiter started shooting them barely veiled dirty looks as they hovered over the empty table. So he'd suggested coffee and dessert at Stomping Grounds, and they'd lingered over caramel cake and French press coffee there for another hour and a half. Conversation with her came so easily. He hadn't felt such an instant kinship with anyone in . . . well, ever, really. But it didn't feel like he'd thought it would. It felt more like finding a long-lost sister. Or a best friend he'd never met before now. Which confused him, after so many months of crushing on her.

By the time he walked her back to her apartment at nearly midnight, he was so mixed up he had no clue what to say, or how to act. In his heart of hearts, he'd hoped he might eventually find someone to be with. That he might have a life beyond work and taking care of his father. He'd always known, deep down, that she wasn't the one, but . . . but, but, but.

But she was a dream. And now she's a person.

How pathetic was it that he didn't know what to do with that?

Solari stopped outside her door and gave a happy sigh. "I've had a wonderful time tonight, Nat. Thank you so much."

"Thank *you* for paying my way," he said. She laughed, and he smiled around the hollow place in his chest. "I had a great time too."

Silence fell. She peered up at him with a strange, assessing expression on her face. Like she could see through his skull. His heartbeat hammered in his ears. *Please don't kiss me.*

The thought was so opposite from how he'd felt a few hours ago, he almost laughed.

She glanced away, one hand opening the zipper on her purse. When she looked up again, her keys in her hand and a knowing sympathy in her eyes, he knew she'd figured him out. "I like you very much, Nat. I think we can be great friends. Don't you agree?"

He nodded, relief and sorrow and happiness tangled into a choking knot in his throat. "For sure."

She smiled. The sight still sent a zing through his blood, though it was less sharp than before. When she wrapped her arms around his waist and hugged him, the longing ache that had been fading all night eased a little bit more.

This wasn't what he'd hoped for, another lifetime ago at the beginning of the evening. But maybe it was better.

He slept badly, woke up late, and arrived on set Tuesday morning barely in time for makeup. Suz took one look at his face and for once in her life got to work without asking any questions. Nat was relieved. In the space of a day, Solari had transformed from dream girl to real-life friend. It was gorgeous and sad at the same time, and left him with a hopeless tangle of mixed feelings he couldn't even begin to sort out. The thought of talking it all over with Suz during makeup made him shudder.

Suz worked fast. Barely an hour later, Nat left the trailer transformed into his werewolf alter ego. With fifteen extra minutes before he was supposed to be on set, he decided to take a chance and head over to see Solari. Now that he'd had some time to think, he wanted to make sure she knew he'd gotten over his crush on her. He didn't want that to come between them.

He slowed his pace when he heard Solari's voice from inside her trailer. It took him a second to realize she was talking on the phone. He couldn't make out what she was saying, but her tone was sharp with anger. He lingered out of sight, wondering what to do. Hanging around felt a little creepy, even though he wasn't really trying to listen.

He'd nearly made up his mind to head on over to the set and try to catch up with her later, when footsteps crunched over the gravel surrounding the trailer. By the time he realized the sound was coming toward him, it was too late to pretend he hadn't been lurking.

Rafael rounded the end of the trailer and stopped cold when he saw Nat. "Nat. Hi."

"Hi." Nat shoved his hands in his jacket pockets and hunched his shoulders. "I came to talk to Solari, but . . ." He trailed off. The one-sided argument coming through the wall spoke for itself.

"Oh. Yeah, that's . . . Um. They fight on the phone pretty much every day."

Okay. Nat frowned. "Who's she fighting with?"

Rafael regarded him with the air of someone trying to make up his mind. "Look, I know this is none of my business. But Solari isn't really available."

Nat stared. "Huh?"

"I mean, she's already seeing someone. She's in a long-term relationship."

Guess that answers my question. Nat let out a soft laugh. "Thanks for letting me know. But it doesn't matter. We sort of decided we're friends, not anything else."

Surprise and relief flowed through Rafael's dark eyes. "Oh. Well. Good, then. That's good."

"So you thought she was playing me? And you wanted me to know the truth?"

Rafael's cheeks flushed pink. "Like I said, I know it's not my business. But it's not right for her to take advantage of your feelings like that. I mean, I'm glad it didn't turn out that way, but. Yeah." He rubbed a hand over the short hair at the back of his head and peered at Nat with a sheepish half smile.

A sudden attraction zipped across Nat's nerve endings. Flustered Rafael was *too* damn cute. Nat grinned as best he could with the prosthetics on. "Thanks for looking out for me. Even if you didn't really need to." The words emerged slightly growly, the way they always did when he had in his wolf fangs.

"No problem." Rafael tilted his head sideways. His eyes narrowed. "Are you gonna keep dating her?" He bracketed *dating* with air quotes.

"I wouldn't call it *dating*, but I guess we'll keep hanging out." Nat scanned Rafael's face, trying to figure out what his deal was. "Why does it matter? What aren't you telling me?"

"Nothing. It doesn't matter."

It was all Nat could do not to roll his eyes. Rafael might as well have *I'm lying* BeDazzled on his forehead.

"Okay, then." Nat patted Rafael's arm. "Don't worry so much, Rafael. I don't think I'm going to be a threat to her boyfriend. Or whoever."

A strange expression crossed Rafael's features. "Uh . . ."

Before Nat could decide what *that* meant, the alarm popped up on his phone, reminding him he needed to be on set in a few minutes. "I gotta go. I'm due on set. Tell Solari I said hi, okay? See you later."

"Yeah. See you."

He walked away, heading for the set. He didn't look back, but he could feel Rafael watching him.

Normally, he hated being stared at. He tended to imagine ax murderers rather than admirers. This time, though, he didn't mind. Partly because he wasn't immune to good-looking men, but mostly because his brain was occupied with what Rafael had said, and even more with what he *hadn't* said. He obviously knew some sort of secret. Nat was dying to know what it was.

He couldn't help laughing at himself, despite the weird sidelong glances it earned him from the other cast and crew hurrying by. At least he'd shed the helpless, hopeless ache that had held him captive for months. Plus he'd gotten a new friend out of it, which was cool. He'd never made friends easily, and it was a relief to know he could develop an instant rapport with someone, particularly somebody as famous and—face it—out of his league as Solari.

While he made his way to the set, he thought about why she hadn't told him she was in a relationship. He figured he knew. She'd asked *him* out, plus he'd heard her arguing with her person— boyfriend? girlfriend? Nat had no clue—which meant all must not be well between them.

Shit. He'd almost been the Other Man. *So* not good.

Duh. That's what Rafael was trying to save you from.

The mental image of Rafael, all embarrassed and blushing, made Nat smile. The man might be a buttinski, but his heart was in the right place. And he really was awfully cute.

Nat was only a few steps short of the set when his cell phone vibrated. He pulled it out of his pocket and glanced at the screen. Maybe he could let it go to voice mail.

It was his father.

Fuck.

He almost ignored it anyway. His dad never called him for anything good, and rarely for anything important.

But the memory of his father's injury and the constant fear of another one made Nat swipe Answer. "What's up, Dad?"

"Nat. I need you to do something for me."

"I'm at work. You know that." He stopped and lowered his voice, even though he was nowhere near the entrance to the indoor set. "I'll help you out if it can wait."

Silence. Ragged breathing came through the phone. "For how long?"

"Until I'm off today. At least six tonight, I guess."

"I can't wait that long."

Christ. Frustrated, Nat rubbed the back of his neck. "Well, I'm sorry, but you're gonna *have* to wait, 'cause I can't just leave work for . . ." He stopped, realizing he didn't know. "What do you need, exactly?"

Another stretch of tense quiet. A familiar dread coiled in Nat's stomach. He had a feeling he knew what he was about to hear.

"I'm out of Vicodin," his dad said, confirming Nat's hunch. "And Dr. Takoda wouldn't give me a refill. He called in something else instead. I can't remember what, but he said it's not as strong. That's no good, Nat. I need you to get me some more Vicodin."

Nat closed his eyes. "No."

"Nat—"

"I said *no*." Opening his eyes again, Nat pushed his free hand into his jeans pocket so he couldn't pinch the bridge of his nose or run his fingers through his hair or do anything else to mess up Suz's hard work. "What the hell do you expect me to do, Dad? Do you think I'm gonna go to the ER or something and tell them my fucking back hurts and hope they'll give me a prescription so I can hand the meds over to you?"

"You could."

His father's voice sounded so hopeful. It made Nat angry and sad. "No, I couldn't. Even if I could, I won't."

"Please, son. *Please*. I'm hurting so bad." Pleading now. Tears in his voice.

God, Nat was so damn *tired* of it all. "I'm sorry you're hurting. I really am. But I'm not gonna help you get more drugs you shouldn't have. You take way too many as it is. That's why you keep running out early. And that's probably why Dr. Takoda's giving you something different this time." He drew a deep breath, his throat tight and aching. "You need me to go pick up your new prescription?"

A put-out sigh floated through the phone. "No. Mrs. Hawk's doing it."

Thank God for small favors. "Okay, good. The heating pad's under the bathroom sink. Try that. Take some ibuprofen in the meantime, or a Flexeril. Try to relax. Call and make an appointment with the doc to talk over your pain control plan. If I can't take you, I'll find someone who can. Okay?"

"All right." Voice low, expressionless, defeated. When he spoke like that, Nat was never sure whether it was real or a guilt trip. "See you tonight." The phone clicked off.

Nat sighed as he stuck his phone in his pocket. He hated for his father to be in pain, but he couldn't enable his addiction. There had to be a better way. Sadly, Nat had never had any luck getting his dad to agree to talk to a psych doc about his addiction, or his depression. Hell, he refused to even admit those problems existed. Like they weren't scrawled all over him for the whole world to see.

Nat laughed, low and sharp. "God, what a fucking mess."

The door to the soundstage opened. Levi Pritchard emerged, his phone pressed to his ear. He nodded at Nat and strode past. Nat gave him an awkward wave. Did Levi Pritchard even know who he was? Or was he just being friendly?

Does it matter?

No, not really. And Nat needed to stop lingering outside and get on in there before somebody came looking for him.

He glanced around. Not ten feet away, Rafael stood rooted to the ground, staring at him.

CHAPTER FOUR

Rafael wasn't sure what exactly he'd halfway overheard, but whatever it was, it had lit a fire in Nat Horn's pale eyes. Standing there statue-still, fury and frustration pulsing from him in near-visible waves, he seemed ready to attack. Rafael had to fight the urge to back up.

"What the hell are you staring at?" Nat's voice was a growl. Coming from the werewolf prosthetics and makeup, it sent a hard chill down Rafael's back.

He cleared his throat. "Sorry, I didn't mean to, I was only—"

"It's rude to eavesdrop. Didn't anybody ever tell you that?"

Rafael's heartbeat kicked into high gear. Was it wrong that he found angry Nat scary-hot? "I'm sorry. I didn't intend to overhear. In fact, I really didn't hear that much, but . . ." Curiosity and concern pushed through the mingled fear and attraction churning inside him. "Listen, I know it's none of my business—" he seemed to be saying that a lot lately; his dad would tell him he should listen to himself "—but are you okay?"

Surprise widened Nat's eyes for a second before the suspicion returned. "I'm fine. And I need to get on set." With that, he swiveled and stalked into the soundstage.

Rafael watched until he was out of sight, then stood there for a few more minutes, thinking. Solari was going to kill him when she found out he'd told Nat her secret—well, part of it, anyway; he'd never out her without her permission—but he couldn't be sorry about it. He hadn't heard much besides "Dad" and "no," but he couldn't shake the helpless anger and sadness in Nat's voice. Whatever was going on in Nat's private life, it was obviously painful and difficult. Maybe he was really over his crush on Solari and maybe not. Hopefully he was. But if he wasn't, he didn't need the extra heartache of getting close to her and *then* finding out he couldn't be with her the way he wanted.

Rafael smiled, imagining what his dad would say. *You shouldn't go around poking into other people's business, RayRay. One day you'll get nosy with the wrong person and end up getting hurt.*

So far his dad's dire predictions hadn't come true. But he knew he got overly inquisitive sometimes. He couldn't help it. People fascinated him. Always had. He wanted to know why one person smiled and hummed a song, while another sat hunched and silent, and a third fidgeted and darted nervous glances all around. While other children on his block growing up had wished for the power to fly, or for super strength, he'd longed to read minds. To sift through people's innermost thoughts and learn what made them who they were.

His mother had told him once that his desire to know his fellow human beings on the deepest possible level was what made him a good director, because it gave him the drive to bring out the story inside each person. Maybe that was true. He liked to think it was.

"Rafael?"

Startled, he spun to face Solari, who'd walked right up to him while he was lost in thought. "Oh. Hi. Sorry, I was thinking."

She arched one perfectly groomed brow. "I can see that. Is everything all right?"

"Oh, yeah. Fine." He sucked his bottom lip into his mouth, then let it go with a pop. "I told Nat that you're seeing someone."

Shock drained the color from her cheeks. "You *what*?"

"Don't worry, I didn't tell him *who*. Only that you were seeing *somebody*." He peered from side to side. A few of the crew members were milling around, but no one was close enough to hear their conversation. "The real secret is safe."

She blew out a breath. Anger flashed in her eyes. "Still, that wasn't for you to reveal. What the hell were you thinking?"

He lifted his chin and straightened his shoulders. "It wasn't fair for him not to know. But he told me you guys were just friends anyhow."

"Yes." Unmistakable guilt settled over her features. "I wouldn't have let it go far enough for Nat to get hurt, you know. I *like* him. He's very sweet. And very good company too."

That made Rafael feel better about the whole thing. He almost asked why Solari had asked Nat out in the first place, then stopped. He didn't want to push his luck and end up getting fired. "Yeah. He is."

A gust of damp wind moaned along the walkway, and Solari pulled her sweater tighter around herself. "Well. I need to be on set soon. Would you mind getting me a coffee?"

"Sure thing. I'll meet you on the set."

She gave him a halfhearted smile, turned, and strode toward the soundstage where Nat had gone a few minutes ago. Rafael headed for craft services, his mind whirling. Every time his thoughts settled, he found himself focusing on Nat's face.

While Solari worked, Rafael waited in the shadows at the back and watched Nat. Studied the way his presence filled the set during the couple of minutes he was on camera. The man was *born* to be on film.

Rafael edged forward a few steps so he could see better. Nat was slouched on a sofa right now, but even in stillness he projected a sense of leashed energy that drew the attention of everyone around him.

He's my lead. I need him in my film. He had no idea the true extent of Nat's acting ability, since his character never spoke. But anyone who conveyed as much as he did with nothing but a glare and the curl of a lip under werewolf prosthetics could likely carry any role Rafael handed him. And Rafael's gut said that the character at the center of *Inside* was practically tailor-made for Nat.

Rafael lost track of Nat when he left the set, but spotted him again—minus the makeup—in craft services a few hours later, hunched over his lunch tray at one of the handful of two-person tables in the huge room. He couldn't have said *leave me alone* any more clearly if he'd hung a sign around his neck.

Because nobody ever got anywhere in Hollywood by respecting boundaries, Rafael carried his tray straight to Nat's table and planted himself in the chair across from him. "Hi. Mind if I sit here?"

Nat's slow, penetrating stare drilled holes in Rafael's skull for seven long seconds. Finally, Nat shrugged and dropped his gaze to his half-eaten vegetables and rice. "Free country."

So Nat was going to be a tough nut to crack. Fine. Rafael didn't back down from challenges.

He flashed his widest, brightest grin as he stirred his vegan chili. "Look, I know you're probably pretty busy. But I've been trying to find someone to show me the local sights, and—"

"The *sights*?" Nat snickered, pale eyes fixing on Rafael's face with a strange blend of amusement and disdain. "C'mon, man. You've been here long enough to have seen our, like, two tourist attractions, other than the show. *Wolf's Landing is* the sights."

Rafael spooned chili into his mouth and reminded himself that Nat was having troubles he couldn't even imagine. Literally, since he hadn't been able to work out what the phone conversation he'd sort of overheard had been about. "See, that's the thing. I'm not interested in the usual tourist stuff. I want to see the spots only the locals know about." He planted his elbows on the plastic table and leaned forward, gazing deep into Nat's strange, intense wolf eyes. "You said you're from here."

"Yep." Nat speared a slice of squash on his fork, popped it into his mouth, and chewed, watching Rafael the whole time.

Since Nat didn't seem likely to say anything else without a little help, Rafael decided to prod. "Okay. Great. So, would you be willing to show me around? I'd be really grateful if you would." He smiled again, making sure his dimples showed. His mom always said no one could resist his dimples.

"If you're looking for fancy shops or restaurants or stuff like that, ask somebody else." Nat lifted his water bottle to his lips and drank. His throat worked with each swallow. He plunked the water bottle on the table and licked his lips, an unconsciously sexy movement that sent shockwaves through Rafael's insides. "But I know the woods like the back of my hand. I can take you to places nobody else knows. If that's what you really want."

Rafael was a city kid. Hollywood ran like glitter in his blood. The sum total of his wilderness knowledge came from the shoots he'd been on with this show. Which made him wonder why he didn't even hesitate to answer. "That sounds perfect. When's your next day off? I'll bring lunch, and you can show me your favorite out-of-the-way spot in the woods."

For a few endless seconds, Nat stared at him like he'd offered to shove rusty nails up his nose. Rafael widened his eyes and tried to look like a harmless Hollywood transient. Which he was, when it came right down to it.

Finally, Nat turned his attention back to his lunch. "I'm off Sunday."

"Solari's got a night shoot, which means I'm working that night too, but I'm free during the day."

Nat nodded and pushed his food around the plate with his fork. "Okay. We can meet up at Hobb's Park. You know where that is?"

"Yeah." He didn't, actually, but he could Google it easily enough. "What time?"

"Ten in the morning work for you?"

"Sure." It was a little early, considering how late he'd be up the night before working on his Kickstarter site for *Inside*, but he wasn't about to say so. "Where're we going? Anything I need to bring, other than the food?"

"A waterproof jacket with a hood, since it'll probably rain at some point. And make sure you wear good hiking boots." Nat grinned, softening his sharp features and turning his face from intriguingly attractive to downright handsome. "I hope you're up for a few hours of off-trail exploring, Hollywood."

When Rafael was twelve, he'd visited Muir Woods with his parents. That was the extent of his travels into the wild. But he'd never in his life backed down from a dare, and he wasn't going to start now.

"Bring it on, Wolfman. I'm up for whatever you've got." He tore open a packet of saltines and crumbled them into his chili, holding Nat's gaze with deliberate challenge.

Nat's grin twisted into a smirk, his eyes glittering with wicked glee. "This is gonna be fun."

Struggling uphill in Nat's wake five days later, Rafael finally understood the evil gleam he'd seen in Nat's eyes during that fateful lunch. Evidently, Nat's idea of fun involved inventing a path through the thickest part of the forest, winding up the steepest slope of the tallest available mountain.

Okay, so Bayside Ridge was more of a hill than an actual mountain. But it had looked so pretty and innocuous from town. He'd never have guessed the blanket of evergreens hid so many rocks, deep grooves, and various other obstacles blocking the barely visible path.

Rafael's hiking boots—never used before today—slipped in the slick detritus on the forest floor for about the millionth time. Nat stopped and peered over his shoulder at Rafael. "Okay there, Hollywood?"

"Fine." He forced a smile in spite of his hammering pulse and the urge to gasp for breath. "This place is absolutely gorgeous." Which was true, even though the beauty was of the dangerous sort.

Nat raised his eyebrows as if he thought Rafael was lying, but he turned around without a word and resumed his breakneck pace.

Shit. At this rate, Rafael might have a heart attack before they got to wherever the hell it was they were headed. "Hey, Nat? Could we maybe slow down a little?"

"Sure." Nat immediately slowed to something closer to a walk than a run. He shot Rafael an amused glance around the backpack full of food he'd insisted on carrying because, as he'd said, Rafael wouldn't be able to do it. "Sorry, I should've figured you couldn't keep up."

Rafael ground his teeth together. *He's being annoying on purpose. Don't take the bait.* "Well, there's that. But I've never been up here before, and you're going so fast I can't even look around. I want to take the time to see everything."

Nat stopped again. He tilted his head up and sideways, peering into the treetops, his expression inscrutable. "Yeah. I get that." He closed his eyes. His lips parted.

Watching him, a strange, tight sensation settled in Rafael's chest. He felt almost as if he were spying on a private moment. Uncomfortable for no reason he could pinpoint, he turned and studied his surroundings. It really was an enchanting place—brilliantly green, quiet, smelling of damp earth and distant rain. Not a single sound other than birds, water dripping on the leaves and ground, and the mournful sigh of the wind through the branches. If he hadn't known the town of Bluewater Bay lay only a few miles away, he'd have thought he had fallen into an untouched wilderness far from civilization.

He drew a deep breath of cool, misty air, and felt months of stress begin to crumble away. "I can see why you love it here. It's incredibly peaceful. Like you're the only person in the world, and no one else has ever set foot here."

"Exactly." Nat turned, a crooked smile on his face. "Wait till we get to the top. You can see forever."

Rafael squinted upward. The slope climbed up, and up, and up some more, the trees marching on until they blurred together. Yikes. "Sounds awesome. How much farther?"

Nat laughed, the sound as low and measured as his speech. "Not as far as it looks." He tromped the few steps back toward Rafael and clapped him on the shoulder. "C'mon, Hollywood. You can do it."

Rafael laughed too, encouraged by the way Nat seemed to be loosening up in his company. "Damn right I can, Wolfman."

Nat favored him with the big, bright grin that Rafael had come to realize over the past few days was a rare gift. His heart lodged in his throat. They stood there staring at each other for a long, breathless moment before Nat dropped his gaze and resumed the hike uphill.

This time, he kept his pace leisurely, even pointing out particular plants and birdcalls along the way. Rafael found himself getting lost in the serene beauty of the forest, and—somewhat to his surprise— the pleasure of Nat's company. He and Solari had cornered Nat for lunch a couple of times over the past five days, but Rafael had been too tense on those occasions to really enjoy himself, worrying about Solari, about Nat, about what sort of gossip might crop up concerning them and how they—especially Nat—would handle it. Mostly, he'd worried about how he could best broach the subject of having Nat work on the film project with him.

Now, out here, his concerns seemed unimportant. He and Nat talked easily, like old friends. It was nice. Nat even forgot to call him Hollywood after a while.

When they walked out of the trees into a large, open field, Rafael was surprised. "We're already at the top?"

"Yep." Nat strode through the knee-high grass, yellow-green and rippling in the wind. "There's a great view of the town and the harbor from the other side."

Rafael followed him across the meadow. The day had turned warmer than he'd expected, even with the altitude and the stiff breeze. Insects jumped and buzzed around his legs, and the air smelled like grass. He lifted his face to the midday sunshine. God, what a perfect spot. He was going to have to come here again, if he could remember the way. Maybe Nat would be willing to give him directions.

They topped a slight rise and started down the other side. Rafael's mouth fell open when he saw the town of Bluewater Bay spread out far below him, its harbor sparkling sapphire in the sun. "Oh, wow. That's incredible." He pointed across the water at Vancouver Island. "You can see Canada from here. It's so pretty."

"Yeah." Nat climbed onto a large stone sticking out of the ground and perched on the flat top. "I like to come up here. It's a good place to get away from everything, you know? Sit and think."

"For sure." Rafael scrambled up the boulder to sit beside Nat. The ridge fell away below them in a steep tumble of rocks and evergreens. "It really does feel like you can see forever, doesn't it?"

"We used to hike up here when I was a kid. Me, my parents, and my sister, Abby. It was my mom's favorite spot."

Wistfulness threaded through Nat's voice. Rafael studied his profile. "Was?"

"She died when I was seven. Bone cancer."

"Oh, God, Nat. I'm so sorry." Rafael reached out and brushed his fingers over Nat's arm. The thought of losing his mother terrified him. How had Nat endured it at such a young age?

The corners of Nat's mouth turned up in a faint, sad smile. "Coming up here reminds me of her. Makes me think of the happy times, you know?"

"Yeah," Rafael said, though he really didn't know at all. He'd never lost anyone that close to him. Acting on instinct, wanting to comfort, he took Nat's hand in his and squeezed.

The touch was hot. Electric. Rafael's pulse raced. He met Nat's gaze, and saw his own surprised attraction reflected there. The air hummed. Rafael couldn't move, nailed in place by his own reaction to Nat's palm against his.

Nat cleared his throat and pulled free, not looking at Rafael. "Don't know about you, but I'm starved." He shrugged out of the backpack containing their lunch. "What'd you bring?"

"Sandwiches and chips from the Sunrise Cafe." His breath still coming short, Rafael reached for the backpack, unzipped it, and started pulling out food. "I've got roast beef, chicken, and hummus with sprouts." His cheeks heated when Nat grinned at him. "I wasn't sure what you'd like."

"I don't care. I'll eat anything." Nat stuck a hand into the backpack and came up with a bag of kettle chips, which he tore into with gusto. "I love kettle chips. Pick whatever sandwich you want and hand me one of the others. I seriously don't care."

While Nat crunched chips, Rafael took the hummus sandwich for himself and handed Nat the roast beef. "All I brought to drink is bottled water. I hope that's okay."

"That's fine." Nat took the water Rafael handed him. "Thanks for bringing lunch."

"My pleasure." Rafael smiled, suddenly feeling shy. "Thanks for sharing this place with me. It's amazing."

Nat blushed. He hunched forward until his shoulder-length hair hid his face behind a shining blond curtain. "It's nice to have somebody to share it with. I'm usually by myself."

Rafael's chest tightened. He scooted closer to Nat. Only a little bit. Enough to catch the sharp scent of his sweat. "One of these days, when you come to Hollywood, I'll take you to all the best places. The secret spots, right? The ones nobody knows about except guys like me, who grew up there."

"Yeah?"

"Hell yeah."

Nat cast him a glance full of longing and despair. "What makes you think I'm ever going to Hollywood?"

"Because you belong there. You're talented, you're on a hugely popular show, and eventually someone's gonna notice." *Like me.* He kept that to himself. It wasn't time yet.

The color that had faded from Nat's cheeks came rushing back. He laughed, obviously at a loss for words.

Rafael didn't push it. He kept casting sidelong looks at Nat as they ate, watching him gaze out at the water while the wind ruffled his hair. He'd caught Rafael's attention from the start, with his stillness and his economy with words. It was so different from the typical Hollywood behavior. That blush, though . . . That was just plain cute.

Rafael smiled as he popped the last bite of sandwich into his mouth. He'd never seen Nat let his defenses drop before. He found it unexpectedly charming.

Nat polished off his roast beef and pulled the chicken sandwich out of the bag. "You want to split this one?"

"Yeah, sure." Rafael took his half of the sandwich in both hands. "Thanks."

"They make their own bread, you know." Nat took a big bite, chewed, and swallowed. "So. Are you gonna ask whatever it is you want to ask?"

Taken off guard, Rafael stopped with the chicken sandwich halfway to his mouth and gaped at Nat. "Huh?"

"C'mon, I'm not stupid. You've been here for *months*, man. If you really wanted somebody to show you the sights, you'd've asked already." Nat drank from his water bottle, angling it so his wolf eyes stayed focused on Rafael. "I wouldn't have brought you up here if I wasn't at least curious. So, go ahead. Unless you wanted to lecture me about staying away from Solari, in which case shut up."

Rafael let out a nervous laugh. "I think that's the most I've ever heard you say at one time."

Nat's stare turned cold. "Rafael. What. Do. You. Want."

Shit. Rafael straightened his spine and made himself hold Nat's gaze. "I'm trying to get my name out there as a director, and, well . . . I'd love it if you'd work with me. As an actor, I mean. I'm working on a film right now that you're perfect for. The script's finished, I've done some exterior sample shots, now I need my lead so I can get some sample shots of key scenes to put up on Kickstarter. And I really, really want you to be my lead."

Shock slackened Nat's features. "Seriously?"

"Yeah."

"I didn't know you were a director."

"Well. I'm trying." Rafael smiled. "It's what I've always wanted to do, ever since I was a kid."

Nat bit into his sandwich and chewed for a while, peering out over the water. Not knowing what to say, Rafael did the same.

"What about your family?" Nat's question was quiet, without inflection. "What do they think about that?"

"They're great. They've always supported me." Rafael shot a quick, curious look at Nat's unrevealing profile. "Lots of people don't have that. I'm one of the lucky ones."

Nat's mouth twisted in a wry smile. "Yeah. You are." He rolled up the rest of his sandwich half in its paper wrapping, stuffed it back in the bag, and rose to his feet. "You ready to go back?"

No, said Rafael's gut, the part that wanted to sit here with Nat all day, talking and soaking up the sunshine. *Maybe touch him again.*

"Sure," he said out loud, because something had clearly changed for Nat that made him want to leave, and Rafael didn't feel comfortable arguing the point.

They packed up the remains of the food and the trash. Rafael took the backpack this time, insisting that he was perfectly capable of carrying the lighter load downhill. Nat didn't seem to care, his attention focused inward and his previous good mood swallowed up in a gloom that encased him like a storm cloud.

Studying Nat's stiff back as they made their way downhill, Rafael remembered the phone call he'd partially overheard days earlier, and he wondered. He hadn't caught much, but he'd heard Nat say "Dad" at least once, and he'd never forget the sound of Nat's voice—frustrated, sad, angry, and afraid. So horribly afraid.

He's never talked about his family before.

The realization struck Rafael with the force of a blow. Sure, he didn't know Nat very well. Hadn't spent that much time with him. And Nat seemed reticent by nature. But in Raphael's experience, most people at least mentioned their families in passing once you got to know them. Nat hadn't breathed a word before today. Even now, all Rafael knew—well, all Nat had actually *told* him—was that Nat's mother had died when he was a child, and he had a sister somewhere. Raphael's meager knowledge about Nat's father was dishonestly gained and shouldn't count.

When they emerged onto the main trail from which Nat had branched off hours ago, he stopped and faced Rafael. "I'll be in your movie. Why not, right?"

Rafael's heartbeat stuttered, stumbled, and recovered, running too fast. "Fantastic." Grinning, he held out his hand. "Thank you."

Nat shook Rafael's hand, some of the light coming back to his eyes. "Glad I could make your day, Hollywood."

Rafael laughed, giddy with relief. Not to mention the tingles racing over his skin when Nat touched him. He'd been sure Nat had forgotten about the offer. Or simply didn't want to do it. "We'll get together during lunch at work and hammer out the details. Okay?"

"Okay." Nat retrieved his hand, his lips twitching into a smile. "Come on, we need to get back to the trailhead. It's gonna pour buckets in a little while."

Rafael floated along at Nat's side, riding high on his minor victory. He had his star. Now, all he had to do was crack Nat's hard shell, and he'd have a supernova on his hands.

CHAPTER FIVE

After the day of the hike, Nat surprised himself by falling into the habit of eating lunch with Rafael nearly every day. A nagging little voice in his head—the one that sounded like his dad—told him he'd end up regretting this crazy new friendship. That a Hollywood type like Rafael, with his expensive haircut, his gym-rat body, and his happy, supportive family, could never see a nobody like Nat as his equal.

Another, growing part of him silenced those doubts a little more each day, because Nat *liked* Rafael. He was nice. He was easy to talk to. Best of all, he didn't seem to care that Nat was a scruffy average Joe with too much responsibility and not enough money. In fact, he ate up Nat's tales of life in Bluewater Bay like candy. Which was weird, honestly, but hey, different strokes and all that. Nat loved stories about Hollywood almost as much. Probably because Raphael showed it to him not as a magic fairyland, but as a real place, its flaws making it more interesting, not less.

Sometimes, Nat would watch Raphael while they ate and wonder what made someone like him tick. Where did he get his energy? What fed that endless well of optimism? Didn't he ever want to lie down someplace where no one could find him and give up?

Times like that, when Nat got caught up in studying Rafael's open, animated face, he'd find himself stretching a hand across the table to touch him. To see if the heady, exhilarating rush from that day on Bayside Ridge was still there.

It was. Every time.

"Nat? Anybody home?"

Nat blinked and focused on Rafael's concerned frown across from him. He pulled his hand back, fingers still tingling from brushing Rafael's skin. "Yeah. Sorry. I guess I zoned out for a second."

"I saw." Setting his fork in the middle of his half-finished pork fried rice, Rafael planted his elbows on the table and leaned forward. "What're you thinking about, Nat? Is everything all right?"

Nat heard the silent questions beneath the ones Rafael asked out loud, like he had several times over the past week or so that they'd been getting together for lunch. Rafael worried about him. He'd probably figured out that Nat was dealing with stuff at home, but not *what* exactly, because Nat hadn't told him. Had no plans to tell him. Even if there was some actual, concrete thing he could do to help—which there wasn't—hard experience with a former "friend" had taught Nat that he probably wouldn't, in spite of whatever good intentions he had. Nat wasn't about to put himself through the specific, horrific agony of asking for help—not even money, just time—and being awkwardly turned down, then avoided at every turn by the person who'd pretended he'd wanted to help Nat after his dad's accident but wormed out of it when given the opportunity.

Never again. Nope.

"I'm fine." Nat gave Rafael the grin that always made Rafael stare at him like a rabbit surprised by a hunting dog. "I was thinking about the role you gave me. You made me pretty sexy, mister director." And soulful. And fascinatingly flawed. In fact, Rafael's script was seriously impressive. Not that Nat had any experience with movie scripts, but he knew what he liked.

Rafael hunched his shoulders, his cheeks going pink. Which was annoyingly cute, damn it. "Yeah, well. You can pull it off. That's why I wanted you for that role. You have this . . ." He circled his hands in the air, like he wanted to conjure the words he was looking for. "I dunno. It's the way you move. Like liquid. And the way you can stand perfectly still, but still give this sense of *potential* movement. It's perfect for the character of Roland. I knew it the second I saw you."

Nat stared into Rafael's shining eyes, his pulse thumping in his throat. No one had ever said anything like that about him. He didn't know how to respond.

"Hey, Nat." Anna's voice broke the moment before it could get any more awkward.

He turned toward her, relieved. "Hi, Anna. What's up?"

She plopped onto the bench beside him, smiling. "We have some lines for you."

His heart tried to leapfrog up his throat. "Seriously? That's awesome! Oh my God." He felt himself go red, but damn, he was only human. How could he *not* get excited about this? "Um. Thank you, Anna. For real."

"Hey, I'm a winner here, too. I don't do anything that's not good for the show."

"I know. I swear I won't let you down."

The teasing sparkle in her eyes softened. "I know you won't." She patted his hand, and morphed into the serious businesswoman he knew she was inside. "Listen, the episode we've written your lines for is filming in the next couple of days, so we need you on set tonight to rehearse with Solari and Carter. Five thirty. Can you do that? It should only be for a couple of hours, if all goes well."

His stomach dropped. His uncle had him scheduled to work a fishing charter on the boat tonight—job number two, not that it paid well. Still, some months it meant the difference between real food and all peanut butter sandwiches all the time.

But this role could be a real break for him. If he played his cards right, it could lead to more lines. Which might mean more roles beyond Werewolf Number Three.

Real money. Hollywood-type money.

"I'll be there," he said, because how could he not? Besides, he might still make it to the dock in time for the charter. They weren't scheduled to sail until seven forty-five. It was a tight timeline, and he'd probably run a few minutes late, but most clients ran a little late themselves. It would be fine.

"Excellent." Anna stood. "See you tonight, then."

Rafael cleared his throat. "Anna? That is, Ms. Maxwell?"

She peered at Rafael, still smiling. "Yes? What can I do for you?"

He rose to his feet, looking more nervous than Nat had ever seen him. "I'm Rafael Cortez, ma'am. Solari Praveen's assistant. I wonder if I could have a few minutes of your time to speak to you about something very important to me."

Her eyebrows shot up. "I'm afraid I don't donate to anyone's sponsored charities. I can't play favorites on the set."

Transparent horror widened his eyes. Nat stifled a laugh.

"No, no, that's not . . ." Rafael sighed. "I'm a director, ma'am. I have several independent projects under my belt. But I would love to work on something with a bit more heft, and, well. You're sort of my hero. I mean, not in a fanboy kind of way, but in the sense that I admire and respect your work, and I'd like to talk to you about maybe . . ." His voice grew softer. A little unsure. "Maybe working with you? A little bit? Like maybe in an apprentice sort of role?"

Silence fell. Anna gaped at Rafael like she had no idea what to do with what he'd said. Which was probably true.

Rafael seemed to shrink with every age-long second that ticked by, the hope in his face fading into misery. Nat ached for him. Nothing hurt quite like laying your dreams at the feet of the one person who could destroy them, then having that person tear them to ribbons.

After what felt like forever, Anna let out a short, sharp laugh. "Wow. Sorry, you took me by surprise. You have hidden depths, Mr. Cortez. I'd be happy to talk with you, sure. Come by my office later today and we'll set up an appointment. I'll want to see some of your work."

Rafael beamed like a spotlight. "I'll do that. Yes." He grabbed her hand and shook it. "Thank you, Ms. Maxwell."

"Anna. Please." She gently retrieved her hand. "See you tonight, Nat."

"Looking forward to it." Nat watched Rafael bounce on his toes, grinning ear to ear as Anna walked away. His unabashed joy was contagious. Nat rubbed at the warmth spreading in his chest. "Good going there, Hollywood. You're a bold man."

"Thanks." Rafael laughed, the sound high and breathless. "I can't believe I did that. But I saw my chance, and I had to take it. You know?"

Nat nodded. A spur-of-the-moment decision exactly like that had led him to try out for a spot as an extra on *Wolf's Landing*. Which had ultimately led him to here, now, with his first speaking role. Maybe he should be impulsive more often.

Rafael was still talking. "Anyway, yeah, I've been wanting to meet with Anna for a long time now, get her opinion on my work, and see if she'll let me work with her. There's just *so much* she can teach me."

He paused, his gaze fixing on Nat in sudden realization. "Oh, hey, you're getting a speaking part! Congratulations, man, that's fantastic."

Predictably, Nat's whole face went hot. He hunched his shoulders. "Thanks. It's pretty cool."

Rafael's expression said it was way more than cool and they both knew it. Nat stared at the scuffed tabletop, embarrassed. Sometimes he wished he could be like Rafael, all bouncy and openly enthusiastic about things, but that wasn't him. Praise, compliments, and most other sorts of positive attention always made him want to hide. He'd never understood his own reaction, but there it was.

A *mew* from Rafael's phone—his text tone, which Nat found hilarious—saved Nat from whatever else Rafael might've said. Rafael fished his phone out of his pocket, read the text, and scowled. "Crap. I have to go. Solari's not going to have time to break for lunch. She needs me to pick up some food for her."

"Okay." Nat stood and leaned over to check the time on Rafael's phone, using the opportunity to take a surreptitious sniff of Rafael's warm male scent. Mmm. "I should head out anyway. I'm supposed to be on set in the forest location in an hour."

"See you tomorrow, then?"

"Yeah." Nat studied Rafael's face glowing with happiness, and wished he could bring himself to give his friend a big hug. Maybe see how much more intense that zing got with full-body contact. "I hope the meeting with Anna goes great. You deserve this chance."

Rafael smiled wide, the bright, dimpled smile that made Nat's heart go *thud*. "Thanks. You too, Nat. I want to hear all about rehearsal tomorrow." He turned and hurried toward the food, waving at Nat over his shoulder. "Bye!"

Nat waved back before heading off to meet the shuttle that would take him to the forest set. For the first time in ages, his spirit felt light. Buoyant. Like he could fly to the sun if he wanted.

Sliding his sunglasses over his eyes, he strode toward the parking lot. This day was turning out to be pretty damn good.

When Nat arrived at the dock that night—only ten minutes late, thanks to pushing his old truck to its limit—his uncle's boat was gone.

He stood on the dock, scowling at the open water while his good mood from rehearsal dissolved like sugar in an open flame. He'd been late before, but this was the first time Uncle Jeff had left without him.

Dread churning in his stomach, Nat pulled his phone out of his jacket and speed-dialed Uncle Jeff's number. He couldn't possibly have gotten out of cell range yet.

Sure enough, his uncle picked up on the fourth ring, right before it would've gone to voice mail. "Nat. Where the hell were you?" Excited voices and laughter formed a backdrop to Jeff's gravelly voice.

"I was running a little behind." Nat did his best to sound calm, though it wasn't easy when judgment and contempt were oozing like sludge through the phone. "You couldn't wait ten fucking minutes?"

"Watch your language."

Nat sucked his cheeks in and reminded himself how much his mom had loved her big brother Jeff. For her sake—for the sake of her memory—he'd keep it polite. "Why didn't you wait for me? You know my schedule can be unpredictable, but I always show up. And I'm never, ever more than a few minutes late."

"Yeah, well, I got a business to run here, and if I want to keep my good reputation, I need to sail on time. I can't keep paying clients waiting because you got stars in your eyes all of a sudden."

Nat raked his free hand through his hair. This conversation was going downhill fast. "Look, I'm sorry. It won't happen again, okay?"

"You've said that before."

"Yeah, but—"

"No buts." A deep sigh came through the phone. "You ain't a bad kid. You work hard when you're here. But if I can't count on you to show up on time, then I can't keep you on. Sorry, kiddo."

The call cut off before Nat could say anything else. He stuck his phone back in his pocket and stood there staring out over the water while the reality of what had just happened sank in.

He'd been fired. By his own uncle.

Fuck, fuck, fuck.

This was going to mean, what, two hundred dollars less a month? Three hundred, maybe? Not good, either way he looked at it. He was really going to have to nail this speaking part. If he understood the rules right—and he wasn't at all sure he did; the union manual Anna had given him was a fucking monster—the pay increase could change everything for him and his dad. He needed that money, because he didn't have the skill set to do anything but fishing and pretending to be a werewolf.

No pressure or anything.

Finally, when the dockworkers started giving him weird looks, he turned and went back to his truck. Might as well head on home and face whatever passive-aggressive shit his father would throw at him for getting fired from the "real job."

Except, as it turned out, his dad wasn't home.

He wasn't on the sofa where he usually fell asleep—or, more accurately, passed out—watching TV. He wasn't in the bedroom he rarely used anymore. He wasn't in the bathroom, either. Or the kitchen. Or, when Nat went out to look, in the tiny, weed-ridden backyard.

Puzzled, annoyed, and scared all at the same time, Nat stood in the kitchen and wondered where in the hell his frail, pain-ridden father could've gone. He had a hard enough time walking from the couch to the toilet, how far could he possibly have gotten?

The mental image of his dad tottering off into the brambly bushes behind the house had Nat's heart in his throat. What if he'd fallen down the short but steep bank into the creek running through the trees? What if he'd broken a hip or something?

"Shit." Nat ran outside, flipping on the porch light on his way out, and headed for the strip of trees and undergrowth separating their not-so-nice neighborhood from the higher-end homes on the other side. "Dad? You out here?" He pulled his phone out of his pocket, switched on the flashlight app, and pointed it into the tangled greenery. It didn't illuminate more than a couple of feet, but he didn't have a real flashlight, so this was it. "Dad? Dad!"

"Nat? That you?"

It was his neighbor, Mrs. Hawk. He turned and trotted to the fence where she stood clutching an oversized sweater around herself. "I'm looking for Dad. He's not in the house. I can't find him, and I was worried he might've gotten into the woods there and fallen into the creek."

She covered her mouth with both hands. "Oh no, I can't believe nobody called you."

White-bright terror froze Nat's body in place. "What happened?" His voice was a bare whisper.

Mrs. Hawk's worn features softened with sympathy. "An ambulance came and picked him up about an hour and a half ago."

CHAPTER SIX

"Oh." Nat stared at the ground, feeling sick. Why had his father needed an ambulance? "What happened?"

"I'm not sure." Mrs. Hawk brushed her stumpy, work-hardened fingers over Nat's arm. "I'm sorry, honey. I'd've called you myself if I'd realized Jerome hadn't done it. He was awake and talking to the paramedics, so I figured he would've called you."

Relief left Nat weak in the knees. "It's okay." It wasn't, but Mrs. Hawk couldn't do anything about it. He forced a smile for her, because she was a nice person and he liked her. "Thanks for letting me know."

"Of course." She studied him with furrowed brows and concern in her eyes. "You give me a shout if there's anything I can do to help."

Unable to speak past the knot in his throat, he nodded his thanks, turned, and went back inside.

On the way out to his truck to go to the ER, he hesitated with his hand on the doorknob and anger simmering in his gut. Why should he go running off to see his dad? His dad hadn't even called. Hadn't even cared that Nat would be worried about him. It would serve him right if Nat left him to stew in his own juices.

Guilt kicked Nat out the door in spite of his hurt. He shouldn't think like that about his own father. He'd promised to look after his dad. He had a responsibility. Dad would call eventually anyway, when he needed a ride home. No point in waiting around, wondering and worrying. Since he evidently wasn't going to sleep tonight in any case, he might as well find out what had happened.

Clutching his keys so hard they dug divots into his palm, he strode to his truck and set out for the hospital.

The desk nurse at the Port Angeles hospital's ER rose from her chair as soon as she spotted Nat coming through the door. "You're Mr. Horn's son, right? Nat?"

"Yeah." How sad was it that he and his dad had been here often enough for the triage nurse to recognize him? He glanced at her name tag: Pam. Right. He remembered her now. "I'd've been here sooner, but he didn't call me. I didn't even know he was here until I got home and my neighbor told me."

Pam's eyebrows shot up. "Oh no, I'm so sorry. I asked if I should call you for him and he said no, that he would do it himself."

"Yeah. Not your fault he didn't." Nat stopped and rested his elbows on the triage desk, ignoring the side-eye from the waiting room full of people. It looked like the usual motley crew—headaches, flu, out-of-control blood sugar, sprained ankles . . . Hell, way too many people around here didn't even have a regular doctor, which was why the ER stayed full all the time. Yeah, he'd learned a lot kicking his heels around here over the last few years. "Is he okay? Why'd he call the ambulance?"

"Said his back hurt so bad he couldn't stand it, and he was out of pain pills." Pam's lips twisted in a wry smile. "I know, I know. But we can't get in the habit of telling people they aren't in pain."

Especially when they are. Nat rubbed his eyes. "So, he's okay?"

"Well. That's for the doc to say for sure. But I don't believe it's anything serious." She stood and skirted the desk, gesturing to a tall, lanky man on the other side of the room. The man strode over to take her place while she led Nat toward the treatment area. "C'mon. I'll take you back."

He followed her down the short hallway and through the double doors into the ER bay. The place was busier than usual tonight, nurses hurrying back and forth and one of the phones ringing while the lone woman at the desk answered another one. She looked seriously stressed out, and Nat felt bad for her. The hospital—or at least the emergency room—always seemed to run short-staffed.

Pam walked fast. Nat jogged to catch up, and followed her into the second to last cubicle on the left.

His dad was lying curled on his side on the narrow ER stretcher, eyes heavy-lidded and dozy. The lines of stress and pain that had aged him beyond his fifty-three years had eased enough for Nat to catch a glimpse of the strong, smiling man he'd been before his wife's death and the logging accident had killed his spirit.

Throat tight, Nat went to his father's side and perched in the chair next to the stretcher. "Dad?"

His father blinked a couple of times and focused on Nat's face. "Oh. Hi, Nat."

So casual. As if he hadn't gotten himself hauled off to the hospital without even telling his son. Nat bit back his frustration. "Why didn't you call me?"

"You were working. I didn't want to bother you."

Jesus. Nat scrubbed both hands over his face. "Yeah. Well, next time, don't worry about that. Just call. Okay?" He didn't even consider mentioning the whole business with Uncle Jeff. Now wasn't the time.

"'Kay." His dad's voice came out slurred. He gave Nat a slow-motion smile. "Didn't mean to worry you. Sorry."

The really annoying part was: he meant it. Now, after the fact. And after the drugs.

Before Nat could get any words past the angry-relieved-sad-wounded rock lodged in his chest, someone knocked on the half-open door, then strode inside. He didn't know her, and he'd thought he knew every doctor and nurse in this ER by now. He rose, putting on his *meeting the doctor* face.

"You must be Nat." Smiling, she held out a hand, which he shook. Her grip was firm and cool. Reassuring. "I'm Dr. Willett."

"Yeah. Hi." He glanced at his dad's blissed-out face, then back at the doctor he didn't know. "You new here?"

Her eyebrows rose. "I've worked at this hospital for two months now. But I have nearly fifteen years of experience in emergency medicine. I can assure you that your father's care is in capable hands."

He let out a nervous laugh, his cheeks heating. "That's not what I meant." Only it sort of was, not that he would admit it. He rubbed the back of his neck, where the tension of the day had his muscles in a knot. "We've been here so many times, I thought I knew pretty much everybody."

Understanding lit her brown eyes. She nodded. "I see. Well, if you'd like to step out into the hall, Nat, we can discuss your father's case while he rests." She aimed a warm smile at Nat's father when he rolled over and blinked at her. "Sleep if you can, Mr. Horn. Your son and I will be right outside."

"You're the boss, Doc." With a crooked thumbs-up, Nat's dad curled onto his side again, shut his eyes, and relaxed into instant sleep.

Nat watched with a mix of love and despair that cut him to the bone. "I wish he could do that at home."

"So he hasn't been sleeping well?" The doctor's gaze was sword-sharp.

"Not lately, no." He didn't mention that *lately* included the last year and a half, at least. He wasn't sure why he kept it to himself. Probably because he didn't trust people he didn't know.

"Nat? Is there something else you want to tell me?"

He made himself meet Dr. Willett's too-intense stare. "What did he ask you to give him?"

"Vicodin." She moved out of the way so a nurse could push a hunched older woman in a wheelchair down the hall toward X-ray. "Your father has been in this ER multiple times for complaints of uncontrolled pain."

"Yeah." Nat stuck his hands in his jacket pockets. His whole body felt stiff. Tense. "He's not faking. He was in a logging accident four years ago. He had a lot of injuries, including a broken back. The doctor said he has nerve damage too. He hurts all the time."

Her features softened with a pity he hated worse than the searching suspicion. "I know his pain is real. That's the true hell of addiction for those like your father, who started down that road from an injury or illness. They develop such a high tolerance for the drug that it takes more and more of it to help the pain, while they become physically and psychologically dependent on it. An addict can literally be at the point with a drug where they have to take enough of it to make them unconscious before they get any relief from their pain." She crossed her arms, looking thoughtful. "His records state that he's allergic to oxycodone. Is this a *true* allergy, or is it more of a poor tolerance? Because we can mitigate symptoms like stomach upset, and oxy could potentially provide him with much better pain control."

Nat shook his head. "No, it's a real allergy. His doctor tried that in the first year. It made him break out in hives."

"Oh. Well, we can't risk it, then."

An invisible hand closed over Nat's chest and squeezed. He cleared his throat, trying to find his voice. "How do I help him?"

"The best thing for him is a recovery program. But," she continued before he could say a word, "I realize that addiction services are difficult to find and rarely covered by insurance, especially worker's comp. It's the same with other mental health services, sadly." She let out a deep sigh. "There's a support group that meets at the outpatient physical therapy center once a month, if you can talk him into it. I know it's not very convenient for you. I wish there was something closer, but there isn't."

Nat shrugged. "It's okay. I appreciate the suggestion anyhow."

"I intend to prescribe him a muscle relaxer that he hasn't taken before, so hopefully that'll help some. Also, I'm going to recommend that his primary physician take him off Vicodin entirely and start him on something that doesn't include acetaminophen. Long-term use could damage his liver, especially with his continued drinking. Which he should definitely stop, by the way."

Nat couldn't even feel annoyed by her frown. Over the last four years, he'd become the responsible adult in his home. Wasn't it at least partially his fault that his disabled father somehow kept getting hold of alcohol?

He laughed, sounding as tired as he felt. "Yeah, well. So far I haven't been able to stop his old friends from bringing him beer. I think I need a bodyguard for him or something."

Her frown eased into sympathy. "I wish there were more I could do."

So did Nat, though he was grateful for even this much. All the other docs here had gotten so used to Jerome Horn's recurrent presence that they generally gave him a few days' worth of his usual meds and sent him on his way. A new drug, new pain control recommendations, and the offer of a support group, no matter how far from home it was—how long had that been available, anyway? Why hadn't anyone told him about it before?—felt like a splash of cold water on a hot day.

He didn't tell the nice doctor that there wasn't any worker's comp involved. Not anymore. Not after the demon bastards had told his dad he was perfectly capable of going back to work—as long as it wasn't logging, which was all he knew how to do—and stopped paying his bills. When his long-term disability insurance through the logging company had kicked in—*disability*, fuck you very much, worker's comp—it'd covered a fair chunk of his medical bills, but not enough. Now if his stubborn father would only admit he needed treatment for depression and addiction, and accept the available help, maybe things would finally take a turn for the better.

Since Dr. Willett wasn't interested in the whole sob story, Nat nodded and forced a smile. "I'll talk to him about the support group. Thanks."

She patted his shoulder and strode off toward the desk. Alone in the bustle of the emergency room, Nat leaned against the wall. God, he was tired. So tired of the whole damn thing. He tried to take it a day at a time, but sometimes it felt like he and his dad would never get off this crazy treadmill of drugs and ER visits and borderline poverty. If Nat could make his dad whole and well for good, he'd do it, whatever it took.

Because then you wouldn't have to babysit him anymore.

An ugly thought, maybe, but Nat couldn't deny its truth. Not that it mattered, since he didn't have magic powers, and couldn't fix anything.

With a great effort, he pushed away from the wall and went back to his father's bedside.

"So then, Alicia slaps him in the face." Solari let loose a gleeful cackle. "I love this role. Truly, I do."

Amused, Rafael grinned at her. "You didn't *really* slap him, did you?"

Horror flooded her face, making him laugh. "Oh, Rafael, you know better than that. I would *never*, even if it was allowed. Levi's a lovely man. I'd never want to slap him."

Rafael was about to ask her how lovely she thought the admittedly hunky Levi Pritchard was and what her girlfriend would think of that—teasing, of course—when Nat slid into the plastic chair beside Solari and plunked his tray onto the table. "Hi, guys."

"Hi, Nat." Solari squeezed his shoulder. "Are you all right? You look ready to do murder."

She wasn't wrong. Nat's pale cheeks burned with two red blotches, and those gorgeous wolf eyes shot furious sparks. Rafael fought the urge to reach across the table and take his hands. "Is something wrong?"

Nat shrugged. "No more than usual." With that cryptic half admission, he hunched over his tray and picked at his pasta salad.

Rafael exchanged a meaningful look with Solari. They both knew Nat had been hiding something from day one. Some sort of trouble in his life that he didn't want them to know about. Both of them—okay, mostly Solari—had nudged before, asking if Nat was okay. Usually, he said *fine*. When asked if anything was wrong, he'd say *no*.

Today's *No more than usual* was a stark confession in contrast. Maybe it meant he was ready to talk about whatever was bothering him.

Rafael opened his mouth to say . . . What? He didn't know. Something encouraging.

Solari's phone played the *Jaws* theme at full volume. She scowled as she shut it off. "Well, that's my official ten-minute warning." She stood, shoving her chair back. "I'm off to makeup. Rafael, you don't need to worry about being on set for a while, but I think Carter will need you in an hour or so."

He nodded. "Got it."

"Nat. I'll see you later." She dropped a quick kiss on the top of Nat's head, then hurried off.

Rafael tried not to laugh at the comically startled expression on Nat's face, but totally failed. He snickered behind his hand.

Nat glared. "What's so funny?"

"Your face. I mean," Rafael clarified when Nat's eyes narrowed, "you looked so *shocked*, that's all."

The tension bled from Nat's face and shoulders, leaving him slumped and exhausted looking once more. "Yeah, well. A few weeks ago I could've died happy if she'd done that. Now, it doesn't seem to matter. I mean, I like her, she's really cool, but it's not the same."

Rafael was sifting through his brain for the right way to ask Nat what was wrong, when Nat's phone rang. He fished it out of his jacket pocket, glanced at the display, and sighed as he swiped his thumb across the screen. "I'm at work," he growled in the wolf voice that always made Rafael's stomach flutter.

Whoever was on the other end must've had a lot to say, because Nat sat silent and stony faced for several seconds. Rafael watched him, worried and curious.

"Yeah, fine," Nat said finally, his voice low and tight. "I know that. You called in the middle of a scene before, okay? I couldn't answer while I'm filming even if I had my phone on me then, which I don't, because it's not allowed. I've told you that a hundred times . . . Well, if it's a real emergency and I don't answer, call the set and they'll get me. You have the number . . . Yeah, fine. I'll call as soon as I get a minute . . . Well, that's gonna have to do because I'm at work. Like I said before . . . It's under the sink in the bathroom, where it always is . . ." He rubbed the side of his face with his free hand. "Sorry. I didn't mean to say it like that . . . Okay . . . Okay . . . Yeah . . . All right . . . Bye."

He ended the call, set his phone on the table, and went back to pushing his barely touched food around the plate like nothing had happened. He refused to meet Rafael's eyes.

Oh, hell no.

Rafael reached over to touch Nat's hand. A simple brush of fingertips, but it was enough to still Nat's plastic fork and raise his head. He didn't say a word, but his blank face and tense jaw warned that Rafael was dangerously close to crossing a line.

Worry for Nat outweighed any fear of what might happen. Rafael kept his fingers over Nat's and held his gaze. "Nat, I don't know what's going on. But whatever it is, you can tell me. I want to help."

For a second, Nat's mask dropped. His white-blue eyes shone with a soul-deep weariness that hurt Rafael's heart. Then the walls slammed back into place. He pulled his hand away, rose and snatched up his phone in one fluid movement, and strode off, his long legs eating up the distance before Rafael could process what was happening.

"Shit." With a brief, mournful thought for his unfinished lunch, Rafael jumped up and jogged after Nat.

He caught up to him on the far side of the craft services tent. "Nat, wait up."

To his surprise, Nat actually stopped. "What d'you want?" The question was gruff and clipped. He didn't turn around.

Okay. So he was being defensive. Rafael understood that. As a gay man of color trying to break into directing, he'd run into plenty of brick walls thrown into his career path, and way too much of Hollywood's "what wall?" attitude. It was enough to ruffle anyone's feathers. He couldn't blame a super-private guy like Nat for getting prickly about what he no doubt saw as Rafael prying into his personal business. Which, to be honest, he kind of was.

None of which meant Rafael was giving up. He'd never been able to let people he cared for suffer alone. And he'd begun to care for Nat a great deal.

Steeling himself for however Nat might lash out, Rafael moved close enough to rest a hand on Nat's tense back. He dug his fingertips into the taut muscles, hard enough to feel the fine tremor running through Nat's body. "I know we haven't known each other all that long, and I know you're a really private person. But I think you need someone to talk to. And we're friends now. Aren't we?"

Some of the tightness eased from Nat's spine. "Yeah."

To Rafael, Nat's soft whisper might as well have been a shouted declaration. Hoping he wasn't pushing things too far, Rafael moved to stand in front of Nat. "I want to help. Let me, huh?"

Nat drew a long, shaking breath, held it for several seconds, then blew it out. A crease dug between his eyes, and his gaze was focused somewhere far away. Rafael waited, watching the emotional war playing out through the cracks in the false face Nat showed the world.

"My dad was a logger," Nat began, still staring at nothing, his voice low and inflectionless. "He fell out of a tree four years ago and got hurt pretty bad. He had some broken ribs, a bruised lung, a broken wrist, a broken leg, and several broken vertebrae in his spine."

"Oh my God." Horrified, Rafael reached out and took Nat's hand before he thought about what he was doing. When Nat's fingers curled around his and squeezed for a second before letting go, it felt like a victory. "Did . . . did he . . . I mean . . ."

Evidently, Nat got the gist of what Rafael was trying so ineloquently to say. One corner of Nat's mouth hitched upward. "He recovered reasonably well, considering how bad the accident was. It could've been a whole lot worse. The doctor said he was lucky he didn't break his neck, or get a brain injury. The height he fell from, either of those could've killed him."

Chills raised the hairs on Rafael's arms. One of his high school classmates had broken her neck diving into shallow water in junior year and ended up paralyzed. He'd read her obituary last time he'd been home. She'd died of pneumonia in a nursing home. "How's he doing now?" Rafael got the feeling that was the crux of the matter.

Nat barked a short, dagger-sharp laugh. "He's been in pain ever since. He's addicted to pills, because those drugs are the only things that keep the pain even halfway under control. And I have no fucking clue how to help him." He rubbed one hand over the back of his neck, every line of his body radiating frustration and misery.

"Oh damn. I'm sorry." Rafael fought the urge to wrap Nat in his arms and hold on. Why was Nat shouldering all the responsibility for his dad? Where was the sister he'd mentioned that day on Bayside Ridge?

Either Raphael hadn't learned to control his expressions as well as he'd hoped, or Nat could read minds. "Abby dropped out of high school to move to New York with her boyfriend when she was sixteen and I was thirteen. Dad doesn't have any other family left. Mom's brother, Jeff, runs a fishing charter here in town, but he's never been Dad's biggest fan. So it's down to me. And I wouldn't stick him in some stupid home even if I could afford it. Which I can't."

A deep, fierce love underpinned the bitterness and fear in Nat's words. Rafael's respect for him shot up another few thousand points. This time, he couldn't help himself. Stepping closer, he planted his hands on Nat's shoulders, rose on tiptoe, and kissed him.

CHAPTER SEVEN

Nat's whole body went stiff, his lips slack. Horror flooded Rafael's veins. What had he done? What the hell was *wrong* with him? Kissing someone who was hurting. Who needed a sympathetic ear. A *friend*. Who might not want to be friends after this, understandably. Christ.

He started to pull away, an apology already forming in his head. Nat's arm snaked around his waist, holding him in place while Nat's mouth opened over his, hard and hungry. Desperate.

Oh, hell yes. Knees shaking, Rafael clung to Nat's jacket and let the slick press of Nat's tongue set his blood on fire.

"Meow," went an invisible kitten somewhere in the vicinity of Rafael's rear.

He figured it said a lot about his mental state right then that he didn't recognize his own text tone until Nat shoved him away and backed up several steps, panting, eyes wide and panicked.

Shit.

Ignoring his phone, Rafael took a step toward Nat. Stopped when Nat backed up again.

At least he wasn't running away. That was good.

"I'm sorry, Nat." Rafael studied Nat's face. He was too pale, his lips a hard line and his gaze fixed on the ground at his feet. Damn. "Okay, no, I'm not." *That* got him a spear-sharp stare. Good. Reaction was good. "That is, I'm sorry I caught you off guard. And I'm especially sorry I upset you. But I can't say I'm sorry I kissed you, 'cause that would be a lie. I wanted to kiss you, and I'm not sorry I did it." He paused. Nat's focus didn't waver. Sighing, he scrubbed both hands over his face. "This was definitely not a good time, though."

"No, it's not. I mean, I sure didn't mind, obviously, but, yeah. Not the best time." Nat studied Rafael with narrowed eyes. "So why did you?"

His tone held no blame, only honest interest. Rafael managed a halfhearted smile. "My mom would say I'm emotional and impulsive. I always told her that was bullshit, but now I wonder if she's had a point all along." He peered at Nat, feeling even worse as a sudden thought struck him. "I won't out you. I mean, I know we never really talked about it or anything. But whether you're gay or bi or whatever, I swear I won't tell anyone."

Nat shrugged. "I'm not really in the closet."

"Oh. Okay." Relieved, Rafael grinned. "Sorry, I just figured you were."

"Why?"

Yeah, Rafael? Why? "Well. This is a pretty small town. And I haven't seen you go out with anybody but Solari, so . . ." Wow, that sounded seriously stupid.

Apparently Nat thought so too, because his wild eyes went ice cold. "First of all, just because I don't run down the fucking street screaming, 'I'm bi,' through a bullhorn doesn't mean I'm in the closet. All my friends know."

Rafael tried not to wince. Ouch.

Nat plowed on. "Second of all, you haven't known me *nearly* long enough to know who I've gone out with, and assuming I only went out with Solari because I must be in the *closet* is seriously fucked up."

Crap. "You're right. That was a dumb thing for me to say." *And apparently kissing you makes me stupid.* "But I didn't know—"

"Third," Nat interrupted, because he clearly wasn't done yet and didn't care that Rafael had literally not known about Nat's sexuality until this minute. "If you're trying to say that small towns are shit and Hollywood is *the* shit because obviously a queer person has to be closeted in Bluewater Bay, but you can be out in Hollywood, then you don't know what you're talking about."

Okay, that stung. Rafael lifted his chin and met Nat's glare. "Hollywood's home for me. I love it and always will. And no, it's not perfect. But guess what, Bluewater Bay's not perfect either, even though it's a great place and definitely not shit. Which I *never* said it was, by the way. And if you'd been in the closet, that wouldn't have been surprising, because there's *tons* of queer people in the entertainment industry who stay in the closet because it's better for their career. Or maybe it's not but they think it is. Either way, they're not comfortable coming out, which I totally get. It's not easy being queer in this business, whatever anybody thinks. So it's not like it was a strange thing for me to assume, to be honest. I'm sorry I insulted you. I didn't mean to. But that's how this business is. It's weird and crazy and people do weird, crazy, mixed-up things because we love our whacked little world. Who knows, you might end up doing something crazy too because you fall in love with this freaky-ass life and you find out you'd do all sorts of shit you never thought you would to hang on to it."

Through his whole stream-of-consciousness speech, Nat stared at him with a crooked half smile, arms crossed and one finger tapping the opposite elbow. "You done?"

Self-conscious now, Rafael frowned at Nat's chest. "Yeah."

"Good." Nat took a step closer, dropping his arms to his sides. "Listen. I like you. You're a nice guy. You're lots of fun to hang out with. You're dead sexy. And I get that you want to help, like, *everybody* ever. But sometimes you're way too nosy for your own good, or anyone else's." He leaned down enough that Rafael could've kissed him again with nothing more than a slight head tilt. "Back off a little bit. Okay?"

His face flaming, Rafael nodded. He couldn't make any words come out. Couldn't look Nat in the eye. Which made zero sense, really. He'd been reprimanded plenty in his life. This one was the tamest by far, especially compared to what his mom could dish out. So why did he feel flayed raw?

Nat touched his cheek. Nothing but a bare brush of rough, callused fingertips, but it sent electric jolts arcing over Rafael's skin. "I gotta go to work. Don't get all emo about it, okay? I'll talk to you later."

"Okay." Rafael managed a smile and forcibly resisted the urge to press his face into Nat's palm. "Later."

Nat's wry, lopsided grin came back for a second before he turned and walked away, strolling at his usual languid pace. Rafael watched, a vague ache lodged in his chest. He felt like he'd failed some sort of test, though he wasn't sure what it was, exactly.

The phone kitten mewed at him again. Groaning, Rafael yanked his phone out of his pocket. He'd forgotten all about the first text. Crap. Hopefully it wasn't anything too important.

He thumbed it on and checked the text. Carter. Of course. If he'd been thinking, he'd have expected to hear from Carter sooner or later.

Hey, the first text said, *could u bring me some water? And a protein bar or something? STARVING HERE. TY!*

He paged over to the second text. *Set 4. Sorry.*

A smile tugged at Rafael's mouth despite himself. Sure, Carter Samuels was a big star, but he was also one of the sweetest, most down-to-earth people Rafael had ever met. When you got right down to it, he'd lucked out in the star-assistant department. He worked with two of the nicest names in the business. Not everyone in his shoes was so fortunate.

Now if only he could keep from screwing up his burgeoning friendship with Nat. Maybe nudge it on down the road into something more.

Nice pickle you've got yourself in, Rafey, his mother chided in his head. Her carefree laugh echoed through his memories.

The sense of nostalgia and not-quite-homesickness that always lurked in the background here in this town pounced and squeezed his lungs tight. Bluewater Bay was beautiful—stunningly so—and the locals had embraced *Wolf's Landing* and everyone in the show with enthusiastic warmth. Well. Mostly. But this wasn't home. It would never be home.

He didn't text Carter back, in case there was a scene in progress. Instead, he swallowed the lump of self-reproach clogging his throat and breathed until he felt better. Maybe he was a screwup when it came to being a friend—or finding a man—but he was a damn good personal assistant. He could indulge his angst later. Right now, he had a job to do.

Plastering on his best casual face, he strolled over to the snack table.

The door swung open. Rafael watched, holding his breath, as Nat spun to put his back to Solari and snarled, "What're you doing here?"

She stared, openmouthed and wide-eyed, and Rafael marveled for the umpteenth time at her acting skills. Anyone would think she really *had* just realized the wolf man crouching over her friend's unconscious body was, in fact, Max Fuhrman's mysterious young neighbor, Rolf. Meanwhile, Carter was lying sprawled on the set floor looking gorgeous, as usual. He was the only guy Rafael knew who could manage perfect masculine beauty even with fake blood and makeup bruises all over him.

Solari's face crumpled, tears streaking down her cheeks. God, she could do the realest fake ugly-crying he'd ever seen in his life. Seriously impressive.

"What've you done to him?" she sobbed, gesturing to Carter with one arm.

Nat's shoulders hunched. "Nothing. I found him this way." He glanced backward at her, his body stiff and his upper lip lifted to show his prosthetic wolf fangs. "He's my friend. I would never hurt him."

Nat's voice, gruff yet soft, conveyed the perfect level of shame, resentment, and longing for comfort that defined his character. Good lord, he was amazing. Almost as good as Solari and Carter, honestly. His talent was huge. Natural, if a little raw. All he needed was a bit of polish. Maybe not even that, depending on the project. It physically *hurt* to not be directing him yet.

While Nat, Solari, and Carter finished the scene, Rafael rubbed at the ache in his chest and hoped Nat would still work with him after yesterday. The fight that had almost been. Nat hadn't even been mad at him when they'd parted ways. But Rafael felt deeply ashamed whenever he thought about it. In his heart, he couldn't see Nat wanting to remain friends with him, never mind take it further.

Solari plopped into the empty chair beside him, laughing when he jumped. "You were a million miles away, Rafael. I can't believe you weren't watching."

"I was. Up until the last thirty seconds or so, anyway." Rafael caught Nat's gaze across the room while he talked to Anna, and lost his words for a heartbeat until Nat looked away again. "Um. Sorry."

"It's not a problem. I was only teasing." She glanced toward the stage, where Anna was talking with obvious enthusiasm and Nat was nodding, his expression a little overwhelmed and a lot pleased behind the werewolf makeup. "Did something happen between you and Nat?"

He thought about lying, but couldn't. "I sort of insulted him. Accidentally, of course, and I apologized, and he wasn't still mad at me, at least I don't think so, but." Sighing, he watched Nat smile at Anna and walk off, casting him an inscrutable look on the way. "I really need to talk to him."

"Evidently." She leaned toward him, her dark eyes full of concern. "Rafael. What happened, exactly?"

He shifted in his seat, crossing his legs. "It's embarrassing."

"Well, you don't have to tell me if you'd rather not." She touched his arm. "But I'd like to think we're friends. Nothing you say to me will go any further. That's a promise."

He peered around. Plenty of people lingered on the set, but no one was close enough to hear. Not that they would likely listen in anyway. They had their own stuff to do.

Nevertheless, he lowered his voice, in case anyone wandered over and got curious. "I kissed him."

Her eyebrows shot up. "Oh my."

"Yeah."

"So, I'm assuming he didn't react well?"

The memory of Nat's answering kiss brought a rush of heat to Rafael's cheeks. "Actually, it seemed like he was pretty into it, at first."

Solari's lips formed a thoughtful *Oh*. "What happened, then? And why in the world would he think you'd insulted him?"

"Well, I got a text from Carter, and that sort of killed the mood. Nat shoved me away like I had Ebola or something. And then I . . ." He stared at the scratched and scarred arm of the wooden folding chair, because he couldn't stand to meet Solari's patient, unjudging gaze while he told her the next part and why, exactly, it bothered him so much. "I told him I wouldn't tell anyone about him. He said he's bi and he's not in the closet, and I said I'd assumed he was, because he'd gone out with you."

"You're saying that you assumed he was closeted because he dated a woman instead of a man. Once."

Damn, that sounded really awful. "Um. Kind of."

"Oh." Solari tapped a finger against her chin. "That seems a bit . . . thoughtless?"

"Yeah." Rafael let out a soft, sad laugh. "He let me have it for that. Told me all the reasons I was wrong for assuming. Then he told me I'm too nosy and I should back off."

Solari's eyes widened. "Well, he's not one to mince words, is he?"

"Not even a little bit."

"I'm guessing that's part of the attraction for you, though, isn't it?"

He blushed. "What can I say? I like a man who tells it like it is."

"Because you're smart enough to realize that straightforwardness is a virtue." She patted his arm. "So, you're going to talk to him, then? Clear the air?"

"Definitely." Even though the idea made Rafael's pulse gallop. Partly with nerves, partly with possibilities. He started to bite his thumbnail, stopped himself in the nick of time, and pressed the pad of his thumb to his chin instead. "Soon as I work up the courage."

"Good man." She hopped off the chair. "I'm going outside for a bit. I promised I'd call Gina." She smiled, and it was radiant. "She's flying out to stay with me for a few weeks."

Rafael wasn't sure if that was good or not, but he had to admit he was biased in the Gina department. His dislike was based entirely on overheard one-sided conversations and Solari's big, sad eyes.

He forced a smile. "That's awesome! I'm sure that'll be really good for both of you."

"It will. I know it." Beaming like a genie had granted all her wishes, she threw her arms around him and hugged him hard. "Thank you for being my friend."

"Always." He kissed her hair.

She pulled back. "Good luck with Nat." She lowered her voice. "For what it's worth, I think the two of you would make a wonderful couple."

The memory of Nat's mouth on his flooded Rafael's brain. "Yeah. Me too."

Solari pressed his hand with hers, then strode outside, her happiness shining from her like the sun. As Rafael pulled his phone out of his pocket to text Nat and ask when and where they could talk, he noticed a couple of the crew eyeing him. The boom operator cast a glance in the direction Solari had gone, and stepped sideways to say something to the cameraperson. Both of them then stared at Rafael for a couple of long, speculative seconds.

He bit the insides of his cheeks to stifle a laugh. Maybe a little gossip about Solari and her PA would draw attention away from the rumors about her being gay. Just because those rumors were true didn't mean Solari hadn't tried—without success—to kill them.

He was on his way outside, trying to form an apology in his head, when his phone came to life in his hand and mewed at him. The text icon said *Wolfman*.

Mouth dry and heart thumping, Rafael tapped the photo of Nat in his werewolf makeup. *Sorry I was a dick before*, said the text. *Can we talk?*

Relief and joy blossomed in Rafael's chest. Grinning because he couldn't help it, he typed his reply so fast he screwed up and had to start over twice. *You have nothing to apologize for. You were totally right. Was about to text you when you texted me. Would love to talk. When and where?*

A pause. Rafael waited, his pulse hammering in his ears. The seconds crawled by.

I'm free now, if you are. Meet me in the trees behind the soundstage.

In the trees. Where they'd be alone.

Rafael's knees went rubbery.

He drew a deep breath to steady himself, then typed, *Be there in five.*

CHAPTER EIGHT

From his spot in the shadows under the trees, Nat watched Rafael turn the corner from the north side of the soundstage, shove his hands in his jacket pockets, and start across the obstacle course of trailers and equipment to the clump of forest where Nat was waiting. Anticipation and anxiety churned in his gut. The kiss yesterday had surprised him, but his own reaction had shocked him to his core. Sure, he'd noticed Rafael. Who wouldn't have? The man was good-looking in the cute-boy-next-door way that had always pushed Nat's buttons, plus he had an outgoing, generous nature that drew people to him. The fact that he had no clue only made him more sexy.

And then there was that jolt whenever they touched. But when Rafael kissed him . . .

He leaned against the nearest tree and stared up into the sky, remembering the way heat had ripped through him like a firestorm. He'd felt like Sleeping Beauty, the libido he'd neglected for years brought to sudden, fierce life by Rafael's mouth on his. Rafael's comment about being in the closet had bugged him, but not enough to keep that kiss—and the need it had awoken in Nat—from distracting him all damn day and haunting his dreams last night.

He wondered if his willingness to forgive and forget had more to do with physical need than anything else. On the other hand, maybe he was inventing reasons not to let Rafael get too close. Wouldn't be the first time.

He thought of Lem—his last actual relationship—and snickered. God, that was sad.

"What're you laughing at?"

Rafael's voice was closer than Nat had expected. Startled, he blinked and focused on Rafael standing only a few steps away. "Nothing. I was . . ." He shook his head. "Nothing." Nervous, he smoothed his hand over the cowlick where a weird curve of his hair always showed a strip of scalp. "Um. Thanks for meeting me here."

"Thanks for asking." Rafael stepped close enough for Nat to catch a whiff of his cologne. Something green and woodsy that made Nat think of rain in the forest. "Listen, Nat, I really am sorry for what I said. It was completely thoughtless and wrong. I hope you can forgive me."

"Already did. Remember?" How could he not? Especially when Rafael gazed at him with those wide, earnest brown eyes. If he hadn't forgiven Rafael already, that would've done it. "You forgive me for being a drama wolf and getting all snippy about it?"

Rafael's laugh sounded as edgy as Nat felt. "Drama wolf. Very clever."

"That's me. Clever." Nat grinned.

All the humor evaporated from Rafael's face. He clutched both of Nat's hands in a hard, slightly damp-palmed grasp. And, yeah, there was that electric zing again. "You weren't being dramatic. You're right, I'm too nosy. I get into people's personal business too much. I butt in where I'm not wanted. And I know we weren't technically fighting after you left before, but I felt *awful*. You don't know how glad I was to hear from you today. I mean, I feel like we've gotten to be friends, and I . . ." He stopped, sucked on his lower lip, and stared somewhere over Nat's right shoulder. "I don't want to lose that."

Nat's throat went tight. "You won't." Following the urge growing to intolerable levels inside him, he tugged Rafael close and bent to kiss him.

Rafael opened for him with a helpless little noise that shot through Nat's brain like an arrow. Pulse racing and all his blood pooling between his legs, Nat yanked his hands free of Rafael's so he could crush Rafael's body against his.

That earned him a low growl and a near-painful grip on his hair—Rafael holding his head firmly in place to take the kiss deep.

Nat clung to Rafael's shirt for balance as the world tilted around him. Holy shit. When was the last time he'd been this turned on?

He didn't know. Couldn't even think past the *sex-sex-sex* thumping through his mind. God, if he didn't get Rafael naked and between his legs, he might explode.

Since he still had enough functioning brain cells to know that wasn't happening right now, he tore his mouth from Rafael's and rested their foreheads together. "There's an arts festival next weekend," he managed, breathless and panting. "Go with me?"

"Yeah. Hell yeah." Rafael angled his head up and kissed Nat again, hard and rough and demanding. "Ohmy*God* I wanna fuck you so bad I can't stand it."

Shit. Nat closed his eyes and reminded himself that he had to be back in the makeup chair in fifteen minutes, that Rafael probably had someplace to be soon, that they were on the edge of the damn soundstage parking lot. Not exactly private.

He opened his eyes and met Rafael's gaze. Christ, he hadn't been eye-fucked like that in ages. He swallowed hard. "Me too. But not here."

"Yeah. You're right." Rafael's lips quirked into a wicked smile. "Later, though. Definitely later."

Oh, hell yes. Since the words in his head refused to come out of his mouth, Nat nodded so hard it made him dizzy. Rafael's eyes went heavy-lidded and glittering, and Nat had to kiss him again. Once more, a taste to tide him over.

This time, Rafael was the first to pull away. "I should go. Solari's gonna need me back on set soon."

"Yeah. I have to go to makeup." Nat stared at Rafael's swollen lips and wanted to bite them. Instead, he made himself let go of Rafael's shirt. "I don't want to wait till next weekend to see you again."

"Me neither." Rafael unwound his fingers from Nat's hair, leaving his scalp feeling bruised. "Want to go grab dinner or something whenever we both have time?"

"Sure." Nat felt a big, goofy smile spread over his face, reflecting the happy bubble expanding in his chest. "I'll walk you to the soundstage, Hollywood."

Rafael laughed. "I'll totally take you up on that, Wolfman."

They started across the parking lot side by side. Nat wanted to take Rafael's hand, but he didn't. He wasn't about to invite gossip simply because they had the hots for each other. Maybe one day things would be different. Maybe he'd have a real relationship, eventually. But in the meantime, his sex life was nobody's business but his.

The next week turned out to be busier than usual for both of them. Anna was so happy with Nat's performance on his first scene with lines that she decided to write him in as a semiregular speaking character. Which was great, for lots of reasons, mostly having to do with money. He really wanted a new car, and now he could afford it, if he ever found the time to go shop for one. Not to mention the courage. He hadn't had money in so long that spending it on nonessentials made him nervous.

Totally aside from the money, he got to spend more time than ever on set, both rehearsing and shooting, which he loved with a fierceness he'd never felt for anything else.

A few days ago, that wouldn't have been an issue. Or at least, it wouldn't have been an issue in anything but a good way. Now? It kept him and Rafael apart. And he didn't like that at all.

The most time they'd managed together so far—not counting the usual rushed craft services lunches—had been dinner at Flat Earth on Wednesday. Which had been nice, but not enough, since they'd both had to get back to work after. Now, Sunday had finally arrived, and Nat couldn't wait to get out of the house and spend a few hours relaxing and having fun with Rafael. If that fun included a little sex, even better.

He stuck his phone in one pocket and his wallet in another on his way out of his bedroom, then strode over to where his father sat watching a cooking show on TV. "I'm going out, Dad. I'll see you later tonight. The home health agency's sending somebody over to stay with you. She'll be here in about half an hour, so you be sure to let her in, okay?" He didn't like that the first time he'd hired a sitter to stay with his dad, she'd called and said she'd be late, but whatever. At least he had the money to do that now.

If only his dad would quit refusing to join the support group Dr. Willett had recommended. But hey, baby steps.

"All right." His father peered up at him with a frown. "Where're you going?"

"To the arts fair, with my friend Rafael. I told you that yesterday." He hadn't had high hopes of his dad remembering, considering how fuzzy he got sometimes, but hey, nothing ventured, right? "You got everything you need? You'll remember to let the nurse in?" She was a home care assistant, not a nurse, but Nat didn't want his dad to think he was being babysat. Even if he was.

"Yeah, no problem." His dad smiled, looking so much like his old self that it hurt Nat's heart. "Have a good time, son."

Nat swallowed the lump in his throat. "I will. Love you, Dad."

"Love you too." His dad reached over the back of the sofa, grasped Nat's hand and squeezed, then let go, his attention back on the television.

For a second, Nat hesitated. His father was rarely relaxed and lucid at the same time anymore. Part of him wanted to stay and enjoy it while it lasted.

And how long do you think that'll be? Five minutes? Ten, if it's a good day?

Since his inner voice spoke from long, bitter experience, Nat grabbed his keys off the table by the door and headed out into the sunny afternoon.

The annual Bluewater Bay Arts Fair was always a popular event, mostly because of the lack of much else going on other than *Wolf's Landing*-related tourism. But today, it seemed like the whole town plus most of the show's crew—and even a few of the lesser-known cast members—had packed into Hobb's Park for the festivities. The sun glittered on the strait, and a cool breeze brought the ever-present scent of pine down from the ridge to mingle with the smells of cotton candy, corn dogs, and deep-fried everything.

At Nat's side, Rafael drew a deep breath. "Man, I love the smell of a fair."

"Me too." Nat grinned. "You have to try the red velvet funnel cakes. Frederic Jackson from Cookie Crumbles over on Main Street makes 'em. They're the best."

"Red velvet? Oh yeah, we're definitely stopping at *that* booth." Rafael studied the event guide George Hawk had handed them at the gate. His brown eyes went wide. "Oh my God, there's a film festival?"

Nat laughed at the *what the hell* tone in Rafael's voice. "If you want to call it that. There's usually a few short films, some of them good, some of them crappy. It's not Sundance or anything. But it's pretty interesting sometimes." He nudged Rafael with his elbow. "I'd've given you the heads-up if I'd known you in time for the entry deadline. It was way back in January, though."

Rafael gave him a warm smile that made his insides shiver. "I appreciate the thought. But it's not like I have anything ready that I could've submitted. Maybe next year, huh?"

Nat nodded, turning the thought over in his head as he and Rafael wove through the crowd toward the row of food trucks. "Yeah. Next year."

The idea sent Nat's pulse racing. He'd never thought that far ahead. Wasn't sure he should now, when most days he felt like he was barely holding his life together. But damned if he couldn't see himself coming back here next April with Rafael, heading into the big yellow tent hand in hand to watch one of Rafael's films. Maybe seeing himself up there on the screen as Roland, the sexy, lonely, vulnerable main character of *Inside*.

Not that much had gotten done on that project so far, what with their busy and conflicting schedules. Though they *had* put their heads together long enough to flesh out the Kickstarter page with a target budget and a pretty decent list of incentives to donate. Rafael had high hopes for it.

When they reached the row of food trucks, Rafael grasped Nat's wrists and dragged him straight over to the Cookie Crumbles truck, managing to get them there as two hipster-types left but before the group of meandering older women could get there. Score. "Two red velvet funnel cakes," Rafael said to the smiling girl at the window. "And two iced coffees." He glanced at Nat. "Unless you want something else?"

Nat shook his head. "Naw, that's good for me. Thanks."

He kept his smile in place while Rafael paid, even though it bugged him a little bit. Shouldn't he be paying, since he'd been the one to ask Rafael out? On the other hand, he'd bought the tickets—ten bucks each, just call him moneybags—so maybe it was okay to let Rafael buy coffee and funnel cakes.

Damn, he'd been out of circulation too long. He didn't know the dating rules anymore. Especially between two men. *Especially* especially when one of them was a born-and-bred Hollywood boy, used to life on the cutting edge of everything.

Rafael half turned to hand him the first iced coffee, a green straw already stuck through the lid. "Here you go."

"Thanks." Nat sipped while Rafael gathered his own coffee. The drink was delicious, cold and strong with the perfect touch of milk and simple syrup. "Mmm. Good."

"It really is. I'm gonna have to start making Cookie Crumbles a regular stop." Rafael handed Nat one of the paper plates loaded with hot, fresh red velvet funnel cake, then snagged his straw in his mouth and drew a long, deep swallow. "C'mon, let's go sit."

The picnic tent was only a few dozen yards away, but in the short time it took them to stroll over, Rafael must've greeted four or five different people. Not all *Wolf's Landing* folks, either. A couple were locals. People Nat recognized, if not any actual friends. Unsurprising, really, since he could count his friends on one hand and have fingers left over. Boy, that was pathetic.

"Is there anybody you *don't* know?" Nat asked, parking himself at one of the few smaller empty tables.

A totally adorable blush colored Rafael's cheeks. "People are interesting. Everybody's got a story to tell, you know? And I love to listen." He set his heaping plate on the table between them, tore off a piece, and popped it into his mouth. His eyes fluttered closed while he chewed. "Oh, my *God*. You were right. This is manna from heaven." He opened his eyes again and grinned. "You'd better eat yours before I decide to have both of 'em for myself."

Laughing, Nat pulled off a big chunk of his cake. "I thought you Hollywood-types lived on rabbit food and sparkling water." He bit into the funnel cake and raised his eyebrows at Rafael.

"Pfft. Filthy lies."

"Yeah?"

"Yeah. Cake is good for your soul. We know that in Hollywood too."

Nat snickered. Rafael flashed his sunny smile, then lifted his coffee for another sip. His lips pursed around his straw, and man, it wasn't fair that a piece of green plastic got to have that gorgeous mouth wrapped around it when Nat was sitting right here. He licked his lips.

Rafael's smile went soft and sexy, like he'd seen inside Nat's head and liked it. "What're you thinking?"

The trouble-making gleam in Rafael's eyes urged Nat to lean forward, elbows on the table, and lower his voice to the lupine growl that always made Rafael's gaze turn hot. "I'm thinking this is the first time I ever wished my dick was a straw." He smirked when Rafael choked on a mouthful of coffee and started coughing. "Sorry."

"No you're not," Rafael gasped when he got enough breath. "Jackass." His grin took any sting out of the word.

"Hey, you don't wanna know, don't ask." Thoroughly pleased with himself—also still kind of turned on—Nat helped himself to another piece of funnel cake.

Plunking down his coffee cup, Rafael matched Nat's forearms-on-the-table posture and stared into Nat's eyes with a part-teasing-but-mostly-serious intensity that sent a whole flock of birds fluttering in his stomach. "Wolfman, when I get you alone? You're gonna be glad your junk's not made of plastic."

Pure need flared in Nat's gut. The world spun around him for a second. He watched Rafael's sweet mouth curve into an evil smile and wondered how much trouble he'd get in if he shoved his tongue down Rafael's throat right here in the picnic tent.

"Nat? Rafael? Oh my goodness, hi!"

By the time Solari's voice cut through the sex-fog in Nat's brain, Rafael had already shaken himself into the talking-to-people mode that seemed to come so easily to him. He stood and hugged Solari while Nat was still easing his mind back into the real world.

When she let go of Rafael, she hurried around to Nat's side of the table. Her hair was tucked under a wide-brimmed red hat, and gigantic round black sunglasses hid her eyes. She smiled as she stood on tiptoe to hug Nat and kiss his cheek. "It's so good to see you, Nat. I feel like I've barely spent any time with you lately."

"I know. It's good to see you too." He plucked at the sleeve of her yellow blouse, loose and flowing over snug navy blue Capri pants. "You look cute. Are you in disguise?"

She laughed. "I am, yes. And it's worked, for the most part. A couple of people recognized me, but they were very considerate and didn't reveal my secret."

"Well, that's good." Rafael gestured at the cooling funnel cake. "Sit down and have some of this. It's *really* good."

She eyed it with a deep sigh. "I'd love to, but I can't. You know how formfitting Alicia's outfits are."

Nat studied her tiny, fat-free figure. What was she, a size two at the outside? More likely a zero. And still, a few internet trolls called her chunky because she had curves in spite how thin she was. It pissed him off. The fact that she felt like she couldn't have a bite of red velvet funnel cake pissed him off too. In fact, when it came down to it, so many things about Hollywood and Hollywood-related shit pissed him off, he didn't even know where to start. Even though he kinda-sorta wanted to be part of the whole Hollywood business. Which confused him.

Which was why he mostly kept his mouth shut.

"Oh, Gina's here." Rafael's smile turned plastic. "How nice."

Nat looked around, confused. "Who's Gina?"

Before Rafael or Solari could answer, a tall, striking woman with dark skin and short dark hair strode up, put an arm around Solari's shoulders, and handed her a huge cup advertising itself as fresh-squeezed lemonade. "Here you are. It's sugar-free." She aimed a wide, friendly smile at Nat and Rafael. "Hi. I'm Gina Carrington."

Rafael shook the hand she offered. "I'm Rafael, Solari's assistant. I've heard all about you."

The woman's smile slipped a little, but recovered when she faced Nat. "You're one of the werewolves on the show, aren't you? I think I recognize you."

"Yeah, that's right." Nat shook her hand, trying to work out whether being recognized made him happy or nervous. "I'm Nat. Nice to meet you."

"You too, Nat. Rafael." Gina pulled Solari closer, rubbing her shoulder. *So this must be Solari's long-term partner.* Meaning Solari must be in the closet, since Nat hadn't heard even a whisper of this relationship. Interesting.

He peered at Gina, trying not to let his curiosity show. She seemed nice. So what was wrong between her and Solari? And why the dislike he sensed from Rafael?

Clearly, there was more to this story.

Resolving to pump Rafael for information later, Nat put on his best making-friends smile. "So, Gina. How long have the two of you been together?"

Solari bit her lip and kept quiet while Gina said, "About a year and a half." She bumped her hip against Solari's waist. "You want to tell them our news, sweetie?"

Solari's expression—what Nat could see of it—didn't change, but her shoulders rose and her fingers wove together in a white-knuckled knot. "I'm sure they're not interested. We've interrupted their afternoon long enough; we really should go."

"Oh, I'm interested." Rafael smiled, sugary sweet. "What's the news?"

"Well, if she won't tell you, I will." Gina beamed like she hadn't noticed either Rafael's attitude or Solari's sudden tension, and Nat wondered whether she was a top-tier actress like Solari or if she was honestly that oblivious. "We're going public, finally. Isn't it fantastic?"

Judging by the murderous glower in Rafael's eyes and the downward turn of Solari's mouth, Gina was the only one who thought so. Nat thought he might be figuring this thing out. And he didn't much like it.

Since Solari clearly didn't want a confrontation here in the middle of the arts fair crowd, though, he forced the best cheerful face he could muster. "Hey, if Solari's happy, I'm happy. Congrats."

This time, Gina's eyebrows pulled together a little bit, like she'd finally caught some of the subtext hammering her from all sides. Her smile, however, stayed firmly in place. "Thank you, Nat."

She didn't say anything else to Rafael. Not that he'd offered *his* congratulations, because he very pointedly hadn't. Nat got the feeling Rafael would happily die in a house fire before he would congratulate Gina on taking her relationship with Solari public.

Solari touched Gina's hand. "We really should go, Gina. I'm sure the boys would like to be alone. And didn't you want to see the photography exhibit?"

For a second Gina didn't say anything. She glanced from Nat to Rafael and back again, her expression disappointed. "I did, yes." Her smile returned, way dimmer than before. "Gentlemen, it was lovely to meet you both. Enjoy the rest of your afternoon."

"You too, Gina." Nat grasped Solari's hand, leaned down, and kissed her cheek. "Call me," he whispered, so only she could hear, and smiled when she squeezed his hand. He drew back. "Have a great day."

Rafael gave Solari a hard, lingering hug, and Nat knew he was telling her to call him too. When the two women wandered off, Nat took Rafael's arm and hauled him down to the picnic table's bench, then sat beside him. The plank was small enough that they had to sit plastered together, touching from shoulder to knee. Rafael's whole body was taut and trembling, and Nat wanted to fix it. Wanted to soothe him. Make him feel better.

Taking Rafael's hand under the table, Nat wove their fingers together. Nuzzled Rafael's cheek, despite the people milling all around them. If anyone had a problem with a little bit of PDA, they could bite his bony ass.

Rafael let out a long breath, his body relaxing a bit. "Sorry. I didn't mean to be all bitchy. But fucking *Gina*, man. She's been pressuring Solari to come out for ages and go public with their relationship, and Solari didn't want to. I'm afraid she's only doing it now because Gina threatened to leave her if she didn't. Not overtly, but it's what she meant."

"Shit. Poor Solari." Nat rubbed circles on Rafael's hand with his thumb. "You okay?"

"Yeah, I'm fine." Rafael turned to smile at Nat, the bright smile that made his chest feel tight and floaty at the same time. "Thanks for being so great."

Nat felt his usual goofball grin spreading over his face. "My price for greatness is for you to make good on that fucking straw promise."

Rafael's face went from happy to startled to anticipatory. Chuckling, he planted a soft kiss on the corner of Nat's jaw. "Never fear, my wolf. I will."

And that did it. Nat laid his free hand on Rafael's cheek and kissed him. And he couldn't decide if his heart was pounding so hard because of Rafael's tongue against his, or because Rafael had called him *mine*.

CHAPTER NINE

A s badly as Rafael wanted to prove he liked sucking cock better than straws—and boy, did he ever—the truth was, the whole business with Gina had killed the mood, and even Nat's slow, sizzling kisses couldn't bring it back to where he wanted it. So the two of them eventually finished their funnel cakes—cold now, but still hands down the best Rafael had ever eaten—and sauntered off into the sunshine to check out the rest of the fair.

Nat plucked his shades off the top of his head and slid them over his eyes. "So. What d'you want to do now?"

"I don't know." Rafael slipped his hand into Nat's. The urge to look over his shoulder poked at him, but he resisted. He knew what he'd see. Half the crowd turning away with a scowl, the other half trying hard not to drool on their shoes. People were so predictable. "What about the wood-carving exhibit? That ought to be pretty interesting."

Nat's eyebrows rose over the tops of his knockoff Wayfarers. "Hollywood boy goes native. Whatever will the folks back home say?"

Laughing, Rafael elbowed Nat in the ribs. "Shut up. I'll have you know my great-aunt Carmelita married a member of the Makah tribe. They lived in Neah Bay until they died. She used to bring us carvings when she came to visit. I always wanted to see more wood art from this area."

"Well, if that's what you want, we've got some great stuff here." A rare unguarded smile spread over Nat's face. "Maybe you can tell me which ones are Makah. There'll probably be a few."

"I'll give it a shot."

They made their way through the growing throng of humanity, Nat leading Rafael by the hand. Rafael fell into a melancholy quiet as they went. Talking about his great-aunt had made him miss her like he hadn't in years. Made him miss his family in general. Which always made him sort of resent having to be here. He *lived* in *Hollywood*, for fuck's sake. Born and raised. Knew every golden boulevard and grimy alley like his own backyard. But he'd been invisible as a director until he'd hauled his butt out here to the ass-end of nowhere.

Okay, yeah, he knew how it worked. He didn't have the money or connections to make it in Hollywood without a name or any accomplishments under his belt. A nobody fledgling like him had to leave the nest to soar. But just because he understood it, didn't mean he had to like it. He sighed.

Nat cast him a sidelong glance, but didn't say anything. Good, because Rafael had no clue how to answer the *what's wrong* question in a way that wouldn't make him sound like an ungrateful jerk.

Maybe I am an ungrateful jerk.

Yeah, maybe. If he was, he didn't feel like facing it right now. Instead, he drew closer to Nat, close enough to rub his cheek on Nat's shoulder. The well-worn cotton of Nat's blue Fun Acres T-shirt was soft and cool against Rafael's skin. He breathed in Nat's scent—practical soap and old, comfortable clothes—and felt better. Calmer. More at home in the world.

Strange, he thought, how being around Nat made him feel that way, when he knew what a mess Nat's life was. Maybe his own problems simply seemed insignificant in comparison.

At the tent's entrance, Nat stopped, shoved his sunglasses back on top of his head, and turned to face Rafael with a sudden intensity that left Rafael weak all over. "Hey, Rafael?"

"Yeah?" He glanced at the people milling around. Most ignored them, which was probably good. "What's up?"

Nat's gaze cut left. Right. Fixed on Rafael again, fierce as a hunting wolf. He grasped both of Rafael's hands in his and stepped near enough for Rafael to see the *thud-thud-thud* of his pulse in his throat. "Can we go to your place? After the fair?"

Rafael's heart tried to escape out his mouth, taking his breath with it. He stared at Nat like an idiot, wishing like hell he could actually answer, because all he wanted in the universe right then was to say, *Hell to the fuck yes!*

What emerged from his strangled throat was, "Ah . . ."

"I mean," Nat continued in that sexy whisper-growl that was making Rafael's knees knock together, "we can't go to my place, 'cause of my dad. He lives with me. And I really, *really* can't stop thinking of your mouth and that stupid straw and my dick, and, well. Other things."

Rafael gulped. "Ah . . ."

"Yeah." Nat's pale cheeks turned a completely charming shade of fuchsia. "I haven't gotten fucked in *years*, man. I need it."

"Oh God." Rafael clung hard to Nat's hands and found his voice at last. "You know what? Screw the damn carvings. Let's go to my place right now."

Nat beamed like a lighthouse lamp. "I was hoping you'd say that."

Rafael's apartment was maybe ten minutes from Hobb's Park—if that—but it felt more like a couple of hours. Partly because the shocks in Nat's ancient pickup truck were shot to hell, but mostly because as long as they were on the road, Rafael couldn't jump Nat like he wanted to. Couldn't wrap his fingers or his lips around Nat's cock. He'd have to wait long, wasteful minutes to lick Nat open and fuck him into next month.

He was so busy imagining how Nat would taste that he almost missed the turnoff to his building. "Here, Nat, turn right here!"

"Fuck!" Nat spun the wheel. The truck skidded onto the narrow drive, tires squealing, and bounced back to the pavement with a skull-rattling thump. Nat let out a breathless laugh. "Maybe I should try out to be a stunt driver on the show."

Terror mingled with unflagging desire and clogged Rafael's throat. "Ah . . ." he breathed, both hands white-knuckled on the oh-shit strap.

Nat snickered like the rat he was. "Sorry."

"Ah . . ."

Laughter. Low, sexy-growly laughter.

Goddamn it. Irritated, turned on, and coming down from the adrenaline rush of nearly getting killed, Rafael reached over and grabbed Nat's crotch.

Nat sucked in a hissing breath. The truck swerved toward the tree-blanketed hill on the left of the road for a horrifying second before he got it under control. Thank God no one was coming from the other direction. He gripped the wheel like it would escape if he didn't hold on hard enough. "You. Are *evil*."

"Guilty." Enjoying himself now, Rafael squeezed gently. He grinned when Nat cursed and swatted his hand away. "Follow the road around to the back of the complex. I'm in building C."

Nat eyed the cluster of four-story wood-and-stone buildings in silent curiosity as he drove. The apartment complex was fairly new, one of the crop of housing that had sprung up in the wake of *Wolf's Landing's* arrival in town, with its horde of actors and crew needing places to live. It was nothing fancy, but it was comfortable and the neighbors were quiet. Plus, the price was affordable enough for Rafael to have a spare bedroom to use as a makeshift studio.

"Don't most of the *Wolf's Landing* people like to live someplace more private?" Nat asked as the two of them climbed the stairs to Rafael's second-floor apartment.

"Maybe, but the places that're really private are too expensive for anyone but the big-name actors. Crew and PAs end up in places like this one. Besides, I don't really need privacy. Nobody knows who I am." Rafael punched in the entry code, opened the door, and pulled Nat by the hand into his small but homey living room. "You want a drink or something?"

"Nope." Nat kicked the door shut. "Only one thing I want right now."

Rafael didn't have to ask what it was. Pulse racing, he stepped into Nat's personal space, anchored one hand in his silky blond hair, and tugged his head down for a kiss.

Nat opened for him, tongue slick and enthusiastic. One hand kneaded Rafael's butt and the other cupped his head, thumb caressing the shell of his ear.

Rough and gentle. Passion and tenderness. The mix sent Rafael's head spinning. He shoved a hand inside Nat's shirt to rest a palm between his shoulder blades. The skin there was hot and damp, Nat's rib cage moving up and down, up and down, too fast, like he couldn't catch his breath.

That made two of them.

Nat's long fingers snuck down the back of Rafael's jeans and in between his ass cheeks, almost brushing his hole. Rafael moaned. Shit, he was going to go off like a fucking bottle rocket right here in his living room if he didn't slow things down a little.

Nat must've been a mind reader, because he pulled back enough to stare into Rafael's eyes. "Let's go to your bedroom while we still can. You got condoms and lube, right?"

"Yeah." Rafael grinned. Lust-drunk and giddy, he linked his hand with Nat's and pulled him around the kitchen counter into the short hallway leading to the bedroom. "I stocked up."

Nat's laughter said he felt as excited, nervous, and needy as Rafael did. "So you're planning on keeping me here awhile."

"Maybe." Inside his bedroom door, Rafael turned, wrapped his arms around Nat's waist, and peered up into those incredible wolf eyes. "I make a pretty awesome omelet, if I do say so myself."

Nat blinked. The implied offer hung heavy and dark between them. Rafael chewed his lip and mentally smacked himself for being such an impulsive idiot. Of course Nat wasn't going to *spend the night*, come on. Probably wouldn't even if he didn't have a sick dad at home to look after. Which he did.

Rafael forced a laugh. "Forget that. Live in the moment, as my dad likes to say." He leaned in and planted a kiss on the place where Nat's pulse throbbed in his throat. "And I've been waiting for this particular moment for a while now."

"Mmm. Me too." Nat's arms went around Rafael's waist, hands sneaking beneath his shirt. "So take me to bed already, Hollywood."

And there was that damn sexy growl again. Heart jackhammering against his ribs, Rafael hooked his fingers through Nat's belt loops and led him across the room.

The backs of Rafael's knees hit the edge of the mattress at the same moment as Nat decided now was the time to get undressed. He manhandled Rafael's shirt off and ran both palms over his chest. "Smooth as a baby's butt. Do you wax or something?"

"No, I don't fucking wax. I'm naturally hairless." Ignoring the suggestive tilt of Nat's left eyebrow, Rafael shoved Nat's shirt upward until he obediently lifted his arms, then pulled it off and dropped it on the floor on top of his own. "Unlike *some* people." He dug his fingers into Nat's surprisingly thick chest hair. "Are you an *actual* wolf? Don't lie."

"Maybe." Nat's grin was lusciously evil. "I'm the big, bad werewolf, come to gobble up naughty little Hollywood boys." He lunged forward and took them both down to the bed, teeth digging into Rafael's neck.

Quick as thought, the teasing between them vanished, and the need they'd both been dancing around came boiling back up. Rafael hooked his ankles at the small of Nat's back, clutched his ass in one hand and his hair in the other, ate at his mouth and drank his low groans like honey and wished he could sink right through Nat's skin, into his blood and bones, become his breath and his heartbeat.

A snicker escaped before Rafael could stop it. Nat drew away enough to stare down at him with kiss-swollen lips and glazed confusion in his eyes. "Wha?"

Damn. "Sorry, I was thinking about an old movie quote. 'If I hold you any closer, I'll be in back of ya.'" Rafael yanked on Nat's hair, anxious to get back to where they'd been.

He'd barely caught Nat's mouth again when his lips curved against Rafael's. "Groucho Marx. *A Day at the Races.* Heh."

A man who knew his comedy classics. Hell if that didn't make him even sexier.

Desperate, Rafael wormed a hand between them. Fumbled Nat's fly partway open in spite of the insistent roll of Nat's hips. "Goddamn it. A little help here?"

Nat giggled in Rafael's ear—*giggled*, soft and breathy and completely at odds with his usual slinky, sexy-dangerous Wolfman persona, but Christ, it only made Rafael want him more, and that could *not* be good, right? Definitely not, no . . .

A sharp tug on Rafael's pants tore a surprised yelp from him. He blinked up at Nat, who now knelt between Rafael's legs, grinning. "You're sexy when you zone out."

Embarrassingly, Rafael found speech impossible, what with his jeans and underwear tangled around his thighs and Nat's white-hot stare raking his body, from his flaming face to his diamond-hard prick and back again.

"Ah . . ." he managed, grasping at the covers and wishing like hell he could *just this once* be suave instead of incoherent.

Not that it seemed to matter to Nat. In fact, if Rafael's blood-deprived brain was reading the situation right, Nat liked what he saw very much. Cheeks flushed and eyes heavy-lidded, he shoved off both of Rafael's Keds at the same time, grasped his jeans and underwear, and yanked again. This time, the denim and cotton ended up wadded around Rafael's ankles, his feet resting on Nat's chest.

Nat's eyes fluttered shut. He pulled off Rafael's left sock and rubbed his chin against Rafael's instep, slowly, up toward his toes, then down toward his heel, over and over again, like he had forever to do nothing but that. Nat's near-invisible golden stubble scraped the sensitive skin like a fine brush. Rafael squirmed on the bed, but didn't try to pull away. He wanted Nat to play with his body, touch and taste and explore. No way was he going to tell him to stop.

Finally, when Rafael had started to wonder if a guy could actually come from foot-rubbing, Nat opened his eyes again. He smiled, kissed Rafael's big toe, then wrestled his jeans and underwear off and threw them across the room.

Rafael was vaguely aware of the whole knotted mess landing on his dresser, knocking over a picture of his parents and a bottle of cologne. But he didn't care. Not with Nat kneeling over him, wild and sexy as the werewolf he pretended to be on TV, his strange eyes feral with lust and those long fingers strong and firm as he reached down to spread Rafael's thighs.

"Don't move," Nat whispered when he'd opened Rafael's legs as wide as they would go. "I want to look at you while I undress."

What could Rafael do? He knew he was a good-looking man, but the way Nat was staring at him right now, he felt like the hottest thing on two legs.

Or on his back, in this case, naked on his rumpled blue-and-white Ikat comforter, his legs spread and his dick so hard it pulsed with his heartbeat, gaze locked with one of the sexiest men he'd ever seen while that man stood beside the bed and shimmied out of his jeans. The mental picture made him feel hot and dirty and almost too horny to think.

Then Nat kicked aside his pants and knelt on the bed between Rafael's thighs, and the *almost* became *for sure*. He levered himself up on one elbow, wrapped a hand around Nat's long, gorgeous cock, and swooped in to dig eager teeth into one little pink nipple.

"OhmyGod." Nat whole body swayed toward Rafael like a flower searching out the sunlight. His fingertips raked Rafael's scalp, trying to pull hair that wasn't long enough for a decent handful. "Shit. I . . . I . . . OhGod . . ."

Nonverbal. Oh yeah. Feeling victorious, Rafael sucked Nat's nipple hard enough to earn him a half-pained, half-turned-on hiss. Shit, he could get hooked on that sound. He sucked again, and Nat thrust into his fist, both hands scrabbling for a hold on the back of his head. "Fucking *fuck*, man. *Fuck*."

The proverbial lightbulb went *ding* in Rafael's brain. That was what was missing here. The fucking.

Rafael popped his mouth off Nat's chest and went up onto his knees so fast it made him dizzy. "Yeah. Let's fuck now."

Amusement glittered in Nat's eyes. One corner of his mouth lifted in a way that shouted *trouble* louder than a street-corner preacher. With no more warning than that, he tackled Rafael with surprising force for such a slim guy. The two of them bounced onto the bed in a knot of bare skin, grasping hands, and laughter that dissolved into wet, openmouthed kisses as they lay side by side.

A glorious lifetime later—or maybe only a couple of minutes, who the hell knew—Nat drew back enough to peer at Rafael with hazy eyes. "Where's your lube?"

"Oh. Uh . . ." Where *had* he put it? He'd picked up supplies the other day at the drug store along with some food, and when he'd gotten home he'd put away the groceries, stuck the hair gel in the bathroom, come in here, put his new socks in his dresser, then stashed the condoms and lube in . . . "The headboard!" He twisted, trying to reach it.

"I got it." Nat lifted his head to look, then stretched out one long arm and plucked the tube from its spot next to Rafael's SpongeBob plushy. Which he didn't comment on, thank God.

He handed the lube to Rafael. "Hurry."

The heat in his eyes sent Rafael's words scurrying out of reach again. Not that it mattered. Sparkling conversation wasn't the goal here.

He pushed Nat onto his back. His legs fell open, and Rafael momentarily forgot what he'd been doing, lost in the glory of Nat's sleek thighs, pale against the patterned comforter, his flat belly with its down of golden hair, his hard cock and drawn-up balls.

Mine. Rafael leaned down to lap at the head of Nat's prick, earning himself a gasp-and-groan combo from Nat. Clean skin, a hint of sweat, and the delicate flavor of pre-come flooded Rafael's mouth. So fucking good. He opened wide and took Nat deep.

Nat yelped, his hips lifting off the mattress. "Fuck! Goddamn. Oh."

"Mmm," Rafael agreed on the backstroke. He lifted his gaze as much as he could. Nat's head was tilted back, his chest heaving. Rafael let Nat's cock fall from his mouth—not without regret—because he really, *really* wanted his dick in Nat's ass when they both came.

Glaring a glazed and desperate glare, Nat pointed at the lube still clutched in Rafael's hand. "C'mon."

"Okay. Right."

Thanking his lucky stars for flip tops, Rafael opened the tube with shaking hands, squirted about twice as much as he probably needed into his palm, closed it, and threw it as far away on the bed as he could while keeping it (hopefully) within reach, just in case. Nat pulled his knees up to his chest, lifting his butt off the bed and baring his hole.

Jesus, even his asshole was beautiful: pale pink and tight with a bare scattering of dark-blond hair. Rafael knew people in Hollywood who paid good money to make their buttholes look that pretty. And here was Nat the Wolfman, with his eyes that weren't contacts and his asshole that wasn't bleached.

"Perfect," Rafael whispered. He rubbed his slick fingers over Nat's naturally gorgeous hole, admiring the way the rosy skin shone in the sunlight leaking through the blinds.

Nat watched him with parted lips and heavy-lidded eyes. "Don't be gentle with me, Hollywood."

Rafael shuddered. That damn growl was going to be the death of him. Biting his lip, he pushed two slippery fingers into Nat's body, aiming for the magic spot.

Which he hit dead-on, judging by the way Nat gasped and flung his arms out sideways. "Oh fuck. Yes. Harder."

Rafael wasn't sure how exactly finger-fucking was supposed to be done *harder*, but he'd damn well give it a try if it meant more of this pink-cheeked, breathless, out-of-control Nat currently knotting the bedding in his fists. Watching Nat's face in rapt wonder, Rafael pumped his fingers in and out, twisting and crooking so he'd hit the sweet spot every time.

Nat's back arched. One long leg lashed out, his foot narrowly missing Rafael's forehead. "God. Enough. Fuck me."

The world went still. Except for Nat's flailing legs. Rafael grabbed one slim ankle, saving himself from a kick in the head. He stared into Nat's sex-hazed eyes. "You sure?"

Nat nodded, his hair bunching behind his neck. "I wanna *feel* it."

Wow. Unable to speak, Rafael leaned over—letting his fingers slip out of Nat's body—and claimed a kiss that expressed his jumbled emotions better than any words.

Nat's tongue slid over his, soft and slick and needy, talking to him in the same silent language. He nestled between Nat's legs, his cock pressing against the heat and firmness of Nat's, and Jesus, it felt so *right*. So *perfect*. And it would be so easy to slip down a little bit, ease his bare prick up Nat's ass, and it would feel so. Fucking. *Good.* He moaned into Nat's mouth, his hips moving instinctively, rubbing, creating luscious friction, and damn, he was going to come if he didn't get control over himself, like, right now . . .

"Stop." Nat pushed on his shoulders, breaking the spell. "Get a rubber and fuck me, damn it."

Grabbing the condom box from the headboard without rolling out from between Nat's thighs was a stretch, but he managed. Ignoring Nat's teasing grin, he tore open the box.

Condoms scattered all over the bed. Nat cracked up.

Rafael scowled at him. "It's not *that* funny."

"It kind of is." Nat grabbed a packet that had landed next to his hand. His wolf eyes glowed with heat and mischief. "Bring that cock up here so I can put this on you."

Oh, hello. Pulse pounding in his throat, Rafael rose onto his knees and scooted forward until his thighs hit Nat's butt. Nat smiled, long fingers petting Rafael's hip, and a sudden rush of wild joy left him light-headed and tight-chested. He swayed, dizzy. Nat's knees came up on either side of him, boxing him in, and he clamped his hands on to Nat's strong legs, hanging on for his life while Nat ripped open the packet and rolled the latex down over Rafael's cock.

It was all he could do to find the lube and squeeze out enough to coat his prick. Nat's touch had apparently killed his logic center. No surprise there. Still, the last thing he wanted to do was hurt Nat. So, yeah. More lube. He was pretty sure Nat would still feel it.

Rafael meant to ask Nat what position he liked. But before he could find his words, Nat wrapped both arms around his waist, rolled him onto his back, and straddled him. Rafael let out a surprised "Oh!" which Nat swallowed with an aggressive kiss. Rafael lay back and let himself be ravished. His sex-addled brain couldn't figure out where this was going, but he was sure enjoying the trip.

Nat pushed up on his hands, his hair hanging around his face. "I'm gonna ride you like a fucking bull, Hollywood."

Oh, Jesus and Mary. Rafael opened his mouth to say . . . something. He didn't know.

"Nat . . ." was as far as he got before Nat positioned himself, took Rafael's prick in hand, and sank down on it in one smooth motion.

"Ah . . ." Hardly the eloquent poem Rafael wanted to create to describe the feel of Nat's body, soft and hot around his cock, but he couldn't get anything else from brain to mouth. He grasped Nat's hips, fingers digging into the pale skin there. Nat's ass clenched around him, so tight it skated the edge of pain, and Rafael had to fight the urge to pump into Nat's body like a machine. "Ohgodohgod. Uh."

"Yeah." Nat rose up with agonizing slowness, then dropped down again, his prick bobbing above Rafael's belly. His cry echoed Rafael's. "Fuck. That's good."

Rafael nodded, since he couldn't seem to speak coherently. Nat did the up-and-down again, faster this time, and Rafael's vision blurred a little bit. Shit, he wasn't going to last at this rate, in spite of the latex dulling the sensation.

He wrapped his lube-sticky hand around Nat's dick and started working him with a practiced touch. One thing he could say for himself: guys had always told him he had talented hands.

Sure enough, it didn't take more than a few firm strokes along Nat's shaft, a few thumb-swipes over the pink head, to have him *uh-uh-uh*-ing, his cock swelling in Rafael's palm, his rhythm fast and brutal as he rode Rafael's prick. His pale eyes glittered between slitted lids, his mouth open and panting, his body sheened with sweat. His hair clung to his face and neck in damp strands.

All his usual reserve was gone, and it was beautiful.

Entranced, so turned on he couldn't think, Raphael dug his heels into the bed and thrust up into Nat's body. Again, and again, until he was breathing as fast as Nat, his hand still moving on Nat's cock even though he'd lost his rhythm somewhere along the way. Not that it mattered. They were both too far gone to care. There was no stopping this train now.

Nat ground his ass down on Rafael's prick, a helpless little noise bleeding from his throat, and Rafael felt himself starting to tumble. The need to take Nat over the edge with him gave him enough control for one last rough pull on Nat's cock, a gentle rub to his balls. Nat shot with a near-silent gasp, hips rocking, head thrown back and mouth open. His body clutched Rafael's prick so hard he saw stars, blooming white across his vision as he emptied himself into the condom.

For a few seconds they stayed that way, Nat astride Rafael's groin, Rafael clutching Nat's privates while they both rode the high. Finally, Nat fell forward onto Rafael's chest. "Fuck."

"Uh-huh." Rafael retrieved his arms, wrapped one around Nat's ribs and buried the other hand in Nat's tangled hair. Grounding himself to the earth. To Nat. "That. Was amazing."

"Mmm. Sure was." Nat wriggled up to nuzzle Rafael's neck. Rafael's shrinking prick slipped out of him. The condom came off and plopped onto Rafael's pubes. He hissed at the sticky warmth, and Nat laughed. "Don't tell me you're one of those guys who's afraid of a little come."

"I'm not *afraid* of it." Rafael squirmed as fluid leaked out of the condom and trickled down his hip. Ew. "I'd rather be clean, that's all."

Nat snickered again. "Yeah, well. *I* like getting you dirty." His teeth sank into Rafael's shoulder.

"Hey!" Laughing, Rafael swatted Nat's bare butt.

He got a low growl in answer. Nat let go and stuck his tongue in Rafael's ear.

Rafael yelped. "Stop! That tickles."

Nat raised his head. Mischief sparkled in his eyes. "Duly noted."

Oh shit. Playing it cool, Rafael lifted an eyebrow. "So, now you know my weaknesses. You gonna tell me yours? Or don't you have any?"

Nat's playful grin faded, and Rafael mentally kicked himself. He rooted through his mind for something—anything—to say or do to bring back the Nat who'd teased him only moments ago.

Before Rafael could come up with anything, Nat's lips curved into a smirk a couple of shades less bright than before. "Oh, I have too many weaknesses to count. But if you want to know, you'll have to figure them out for yourself." He leaned down and kissed Rafael, a slow, searching kiss that sparked a deep heat inside him. When Nat broke the kiss, he smiled, his mouth still brushing Rafael's. "That should be fun, right?"

Rafael watched in thoughtful silence as Nat rose from the bed, plucked the condom from Rafael's groin, and carried it into the bathroom. When he returned a few moments later with a damp washcloth, he cleaned the semen off Rafael's skin and pubic hair without a word, then fished his jeans out of the pile on the floor and started putting them on.

"I need to get back home," he said, answering the question Rafael hadn't asked. "I got a sitter to stay with Dad, but only for four hours. I need to be back before she has to leave."

"I understand." Rafael scooted off the bed and stood beside Nat, feeling awkward as hell. Should he get dressed too? Should he walk Nat out? All he wanted to do was cling to him like a vine, but he wasn't sure Nat would welcome that. He chewed his lip. "Can I see you again?"

Nat finished pulling his T-shirt on. "You'd better, Hollywood." He grabbed Rafael's wrist and tugged. "C'mere."

Relieved, Rafael molded his naked body to Nat's clothed one and lifted his face for a kiss every bit as electric as the others. The way they fit together already felt natural. Easy. Like they'd been a couple for years, rather than newly minted lovers who might or might not end up being something more than friends with benefits.

It should've been scary. Instead, Rafael found it exhilarating.

He was still trying to decide exactly what that meant long after Nat had left with a heart-thumping smile and a promise to call later. The thing was, he had a sinking feeling he already knew. What he didn't know was what in the name of everything holy he was going to do about it. He'd come to Bluewater Bay to kick-start his career, not find a man.

Oh well. Happiness was where you found it, as his mom was always telling him. There was no reason he couldn't have a fabulous directing career *and* a fulfilling relationship.

Whoa there, cowboy. Better figure out how Nat feels about that before you build a whole domestic fairytale castle around him.

With a deep sigh, Rafael dragged himself into the bathroom. Maybe a long, hot shower would bring him back to Earth. And help him decide when—or whether—to tell Nat he might be falling for him.

CHAPTER TEN

Nat floated through the first half of the next week in a golden haze. He hadn't been this relaxed in ages, smiling at everyone he passed at work, handling his father with a patience he didn't realize he possessed.

Maybe Suz was right and he'd only needed to get laid. Not that he'd spilled the beans about what had happened between him and Rafael, but the girl was like a damn bloodhound. She always knew.

No, he mused, watching Rafael saunter toward their usual lunch spot, his whole face lit up with his smile. No, there was definitely more than sex going on here. Even the most incredible sex in the world couldn't account for the funny twist in Nat's stomach every time Rafael glanced his way.

"Hey." Rafael slid into the seat beside Nat, tilted his head, and pecked Nat on the lips. "Sorry I'm late. It's been a crazy morning."

"It's cool." Nat glanced around, amazed for the millionth time that no one seemed to care that two guys were kissing at the lunch table. Around the set, it didn't seem to be a big deal unless one of the people doing the kissing was a star. "You got any idea what they're doing over there?" He waved his plastic fork at the temporary stage set up a little ways off, complete with sound system and a cordoned-off area crammed shoulder to shoulder with slick-looking men and women in suits, and shaggier people toting big professional cameras.

Rafael's nose scrunched. "Solari's holding a press conference."

"Huh? How come?" The lightbulb went on in Nat's head, and his stomach dropped into his feet. "Oh shit. She's not."

"She is." Rafael scooped up hummus on a carrot stick and chomped viciously. "I'd really, *really* love to tell her what I think of that, but I won't. It's not my business, and she wouldn't listen to me anyway."

Christ. Nat would've loved to weigh in on the subject himself, but Rafael was right. Solari might be a friend—correction, she definitely counted as a friend now—but that didn't give either of them the right to tell her how to live her life. Shaking his head, he popped a cheese cube into his mouth.

His phone buzzed in his pocket. He was reaching for it when Solari walked up to the microphone on the temporary stage. Gina hovered at her side, looking both thrilled with the whole business and ready to tear apart any reporter who said the wrong thing. Which earned her points in Nat's book. Deciding the text could wait a few minutes, he turned his attention to the stage.

"Good afternoon, ladies and gentlemen." Solari's smile dazzled even from several dozen yards away, but Nat heard the faint thread of hesitancy in her voice, and it hurt his heart. "Thank you so much for joining me here today. I have news that I'm quite excited to share with the world."

"Like hell," Rafael muttered, low enough that only Nat would hear.

Since there was nothing to say to make it better for anyone—least of all Solari—Nat took Rafael's hand, laced their fingers together, and squeezed. In return, Rafael shot him a swift, shining glance that had his heart turning backflips—and made him miss the Big Fucking Moment. He only knew it had happened because of the explosion of questions and photo flashes from the press pit.

Oh well. It didn't matter, really. He knew what she'd planned to say, more or less, and he wasn't sure he could stand to watch the press circle like sharks scenting blood. Watching Rafael was way better. In fact, he could stare at Rafael's ever-changing expressions for hours and never get tired of it. The man wore his heart on his sleeve—or on his face, to be accurate—and Nat found that endlessly fascinating.

Onstage, Solari answered questions from reporters about how long she and Gina had been together, were they "exclusively lesbian," why had she pretended to date men, on and on and on. She seemed calm, but Nat saw the way her feet shifted behind the podium and knew she wanted to escape the onslaught as badly as he would've wanted to in her place.

Gina's voice cut through the chatter. "All right, that's all the questions we're going to answer for now." She aimed a wide smile at the wall of people. "Thank you for your time."

All the reporters started shouting at once. A forest of mics and cameras bristled toward the two women. Solari turned away with her blank face on and exited the stage, cool as ice cream on a summer day. Gina wrapped a possessive arm around Solari's shoulders as the pair descended the steps at the rear of the stage, slipped through the human curtain of security guards, and headed for Solari's trailer. At least Gina seemed to be doing her best to be protective and supportive, which was good.

Rafael grunted. "Well, that's that, I guess. I hope it works out well for her."

"Me too." Nat laid a mozzarella square on top of a wheat cracker, swiped it through the dwindling puddle of salsa on his plate, and popped the whole business in his mouth. "'Uckin' ra'or'ers."

Grinning, Rafael stole one of his pepper jack squares. "What was that in English?"

Nat chewed and swallowed. "I *said*, 'Fucking *reporters*.' At least Gina's being cool about it."

Rafael scrunched up his nose. "I guess."

Nat grinned. "You're cute when you're mad."

That earned him an evil side-eye, which made him laugh. Rafael kicked his ankle under the table. "Shut up."

"Yeah, yeah." He snatched a carrot stick from Rafael's stack and loaded it with hummus. "When's her next scene? I don't have anything with her until next week. Unless Anna switches the schedule around again." He crunched his stolen food.

"Let's see." Rafael let go of Nat's hand and tapped at his phone, which rested on the table in front of him. "Looks like she and Carter have a scene in about an hour, then she has one with Levi after that. I'll make sure she's all right."

"Text me and let me know?"

"Sure thing."

Rafael's phone went *mew*. A message popped up. Nat recognized a tiny photo of Carter Samuels, and his heart sank. "Uh-oh. You're being paged."

"Yeah, looks that way." Rafael's plump lips curved into a wry half smile. "Sorry."

"Hey, that's the nature of the beast, right? It's fine."

Which was true, kind of. Nat liked Carter, and as his part-time PA, Rafael was duty bound to answer when he called. But Nat felt so *empty* lately whenever he and Rafael were apart. He wasn't sure how to interpret the ache Rafael's absence left inside him, or what to do about it.

Rafael stood, shoving his phone into his jeans pocket. "Okay. I need to bring Carter a box lunch. I doubt I can be back before you have to be in makeup, so I guess I'll see you tonight?"

They'd made plans to go hear some band at Stomping Grounds. Nat had never heard of them, but Rafael swore they were awesome. In any case, the reminder that he was seeing Rafael tonight had warmth curling in Nat's belly. "Can't wait." He tilted his head up, meeting Rafael as he leaned down for a quick kiss. "See you at eight."

"Until then, Wolfman." Rafael flashed a dazzling smile as he headed for the table stacked with boxed lunches.

Nat sat there for a couple of minutes, nibbling the remains of his lunch and daydreaming about getting Rafael alone. In fact, he hadn't thought of much else since that afternoon at Rafael's place after the arts fair. Sex had kind of fallen off his radar since his dad and all his dad's issues had landed on his plate. But now it was back in a big way. He had fucking on his mind constantly for the first time in years.

His gut told him that had less to do with being sexually active again than the man he was active with.

He'd finished his lunch and was halfway to makeup when he remembered his phone buzzing before Solari's press conference. Shit, shit, shit. Hoping like hell it wasn't anything important, he whipped his phone out of his pocket, brought up the display, and peered at the text icon in the corner.

It was from his dad. *Of course.* Because only his father, Rafael, Suz, and Anna ever texted him, and neither of the women would have let him ignore them for this long.

He shut his eyes. *Whatever it is, you can handle it. No problem. Everything's gonna be fine.*

His runaway pulse didn't believe it, but his churning stomach settled a little, which was frankly more than he'd hoped for. Ready as he was likely to get, he opened his eyes and tapped on the text icon.

We're out of that cereal I like. Don't remember the name but you know the one. Would you mind getting some on the way home? Thanks.

A rush of relief had Nat's vision sparkling at the edges. He laughed out loud, earning himself a few cautious looks from cast and crew hurrying by. Served him right. Here he was picturing some dire emergency, and his dad only wanted some more store-brand Honey Nut Cheerios. Next time, he'd wait and see what was what before he started mentally filling in the blanks.

No problem, he typed back. *Going out tonight but coming home first to shower & change so will bring the cereal then.* Hell, he'd surprise his dad and bring him the name brand this time. He could afford it now. No reason not to use his money for decent groceries, at least. *Sorry it took me a while to answer. Was in the middle of something. You doing okay?*

His dad answered almost immediately, which made him feel even worse for having forgotten about the first text. *Doing good. No problem about the wait, I know you're busy at work. Love you, son.*

Nat's throat closed up and his eyes filled with tears. His dad really had seemed better lately. More lucid, his pain better controlled on the new meds. It had been so long since Nat had any real hope for his father, he still couldn't believe things might be turning around.

He blinked the tears away before they could fall, keeping his head down as he tapped at his phone so no one could see the runaway emotions he couldn't quite hide. *Love you too, Dad. See you later.*

The band—Rocky Mountain Sly—turned out to be way better than Nat had expected. Looked like he might have to revise his opinion on banjos and violins played by guys with skinny jeans, tattoos, and brown leather dress shoes minus socks.

Of course, the awesome espresso and brownies at Stomping Grounds didn't hurt.

Rafael laughed when Nat woo-hoo'ed and clapped along with the rest of the crowd at the end of the set. "So you liked it?"

"Yeah." Grinning, Nat squeezed the inside of Rafael's thigh. "Treasure that confession, Hollywood, 'cause you won't hear it again. Hipster bluegrass is so *not* my thing."

"You say that, but I see that gleam in your eyes." The hand not clutching Rafael's oversized coffee mug covered Nat's where it lay on his leg, weaving their fingers together and sending a burst of happy warmth through Nat's blood. "You're hooked, Wolfy. Don't even try to deny it."

"Nah. I'm more of a Black Keys kind of guy." Nat bent to nuzzle Rafael's cheek. His stubble, soft as a teenager's, tickled Nat's nose. "I'm howling for *you*, Hollywood."

This time, Rafael's laugh emerged low and throaty. He turned his head, catching Nat by surprise with a swift, close-lipped kiss. "That's my favorite Black Keys song. How'd you know?"

A strange tightness caught at Nat's chest. Like he couldn't breathe, but it was okay because his life—or at least this part of it—had finally fallen into the right configuration. He smiled. "Lucky guess."

Rafael smiled back, dark eyes shining, and Nat's world tilted. He could drown in those eyes and die happy. It ought to scare him, but it didn't. Or at least, not as much as it should.

Oh well. He'd never been one to run from trouble. Why start now?

Nat was still riding the high Rafael's company gave him when he got home an hour or so later. The TV was playing some cop drama, his father's tousled hair barely peeking above the sofa.

"Hey, Dad. I didn't think you'd still be up." He dropped his keys on the table by the kitchen door and looked around, frowning. "Where's Jessica?" The sitter had been hired to stay until midnight. It was only eleven. She should still be here.

"I sent her on home an hour ago."

Shit. Not again. Nat bit back his irritation. "Dad, this is the second time you've done that. They're not gonna let us hire their people if you keep sending them home early."

"I'm a grown man. I don't need to pay good money for some goddamn babysitter to hover over me like I'm a goddamn toddler."

The wounded pride in his father's voice kept the *It's my money, not yours* in Nat's head where it couldn't hurt anyone. He rubbed the tension gathering at the back of his neck. "You okay?"

His dad gave him a wan smile as he perched on the beat-up old armchair. "Not bad. Couldn't get to sleep, is all."

"Oh." Nat studied the shadows under his father's eyes. A familiar worry kicked to life inside him. "You need a sleeping pill?"

Dad wrinkled his nose. "I don't like them. They make me do weird things."

That was true. Last time, Nat had found him sitting at the kitchen table, eating butter in his sleep. "Yeah, but—"

"I'd rather not take them. Thanks anyway." His father aimed an unusually sharp stare at Nat. "You look really happy."

Nat beamed. He couldn't help it. "I am."

A complex blend of pride, sadness, and love flowed over his dad's face. "Good. You deserve that. More than probably anybody."

Touched, Nat leaned forward and brushed his fingers over his father's hand where it rested on the arm of the couch. "Thanks, Dad. That means a lot to me."

The teasing smile Nat remembered from before the logging accident spread over his father's face. "So what's up? You finally find the right woman?"

Nat laughed. "The right man, actually."

His dad's face went slack and gray. "What?"

Shit. Nat kept his expression calm, though his heart hammered painfully fast and his stomach turned backflips. "C'mon, Dad. We've had this conversation before. I'm bisexual, remember? I swing both ways. You know that."

His father's jaw tightened. "It was all right when you were younger, if you needed to . . ." He lifted his hand in a helpless gesture. "Experiment. You know. But you're a grown man now, Nat. You gotta forget about all this gay nonsense and settle down."

It was like with Lem all over again. Two long years, and not a damn thing had changed.

The hard glitter in his dad's eyes felt like a knife in the heart, even more than his hurtful words. Nat stared at the stained carpet under his feet. "Funny that *this* is what gets you out of your apathy for five fucking minutes. Not your addiction or the fact that we never had enough money until now, or the million other *real* issues we have. No, you gotta finally rouse yourself up over me finally being *happy* with someone."

His dad sighed, sounding almost like he had when Nat and his sister used to get in trouble as kids. "Don't be ridiculous. I want you to be happy, of course I do. I just don't understand why you can't find a good woman. I mean, if you're . . ." A heartbeat of uncomfortable silence followed. Nat ground his teeth and fumed until his father started talking again. "Well, if you're not particular who you're with, why can't you find a woman?"

Because Rafael isn't a woman, and he's the one I want.

Nat stood, trembling. "If you *still* don't get why people aren't interchangeable, then I can't explain it to you." He strode to the table and snatched up his keys. "I'm going out."

"But you barely got back." The sofa squeaked in the particular way it did when someone rose from it. "Nat, please. I wish you'd be reasonable about this. If you'd—"

"Shut up." Nat's voice sounded strangled in his own ears. He couldn't look at his father. "I'll be home later. But I can't be around you right now." Ignoring his father's pleas for him to stay and talk, he walked out the door and slammed it behind him.

For a couple of minutes, he stood in the yard, letting the cool night air soothe the heat in his cheeks. This whole thing was his own fault. He knew better than to believe for one second his father would ever try to understand him. Sure, his dad loved him. But he loved his son Nat, not Nathaniel Horn the human being.

Nat only saw now, tonight, how much he'd longed for his father's acceptance as well as the automatic brand of love a father gave his son. But he'd never have it. And that hurt bone-deep.

Aching and restless, Nat shoved his hands in his pockets and started walking.

CHAPTER ELEVEN

Rafael had barely managed to shake off his date-with-Nat-inspired daydreams and get a good start on rewriting the climactic scene of *Inside* when his phone lit up and started singing "Queen" at him.

It took him a second to remember he'd assigned that ringtone to Solari. He didn't think she'd ever actually *called* him before.

Worried, he pushed his rolling chair away from the computer, snatched his cell off the cluttered dining table, and hit the Answer button. "Hey. What's up? You okay?"

"Thank goodness I got you. Yes, I'm fine, but . . ." Tense silence, punctuated by background chatter and music that said she was in a public place. Most likely a bar, at nearly one in the morning, though he'd never known her to hit the night spots before. "Can you possibly come over to Ma Cougar's?"

Her usually calm voice had a frantic edge. He frowned. "What's wrong?"

"It's Nat. He's very drunk and acting belligerent. Oh dear." Something went *scritch* like she'd planted the phone against her shirt. He heard a muffled shout, followed by raucous laughter and a few raised, irritated voices. Solari's cooler tones rumbled against the receiver, saying something Rafael couldn't make out. There were a couple more bumps and scratches, then Solari came back on. "Can you come get him? Please? He won't listen to me, and I'm afraid he's going to start a fight."

Rafael's stomach knotted. "What makes you think he'll listen to me any more than you?"

"Trust me. He will."

A strange little shiver ran down Rafael's spine. Was it wrong that he liked the idea of being the one person who could bring Nat back from the edge? It *had* to be wrong, but the thought warmed him in spite of his shame. "All right. I'll come get him and take him home."

"Thank you." Her relief was so thick he could practically see it floating like a cloud from the phone. "Do you know where the bar is?"

"Yeah, I've been there a couple of times." It was a nice place, a brewpub of the sort he'd expect to find in Seattle or Portland, not a wide spot in the road like Bluewater Bay. "See you in a little bit."

The call cut off. Rafael stared at the impressionistic cow painting on the wall, thinking hard. He'd rarely seen Nat drink anything other than water or coffee. Certainly never seen him drunk. Not that they'd known each other all that long, but still. He didn't seem like the sort to go off on drinking binges. And he'd been fine when they'd parted company earlier that night. So what had turned him from happy, smiling Nat into hammered, bar-fight-starting Nat?

Rafael stood, phone in hand, and hurried to fish his keys out of the kitchen drawer. Whatever had happened, he was damn well going to find out.

As it turned out, he never even got inside the pub. Solari and Gina stood on the sidewalk outside the door, holding a swaying, mumbling Nat between them. His hair hung over his face, but it couldn't hide the purple bruise spreading over the left side of his jaw.

Crap.

Rafael broke into a jog. "Jesus, what happened?" He stopped in front of Nat and gently touched his swelling jaw. "Nat?"

Nat lifted his head. The bleakness in his eyes hit Rafael like a gut punch. Rafael opened his hand, spreading his palm over Nat's cheek.

A bitter smile twisted Nat's lips. "Life's a shit pile, Hollywood."

Gina made a frustrated noise. "He picked a fight with some redneck lumberjack, and the guy punched him. I can't say as I blame him."

"Gina, please." Solari's voice held a sharpness Rafael didn't usually hear from her. She peered up at Nat with concern stamped all over her features. "It's not like him at all. In fact, I wouldn't have thought public drunkenness was like him. I'm afraid something must have happened. At home, you know?"

Fear flared in Rafael's gut. Oh no. What if Nat's dad was sick or hurt? The relationship between father and son was complicated, yes. But Nat loved his dad. That much was obvious. He'd drown in his own guilt if anything happened to his father, especially if it'd happened while he'd been out on a date.

"Okay," Rafael said. "I'm going to take him back home now."

Nat shook loose of the two women so violently he almost fell over. "No. Not goin'."

Rafael and Solari exchanged a puzzled look. Gina watched Nat with sympathy in her eyes. "Solari, should we take him back home with us, do you think?"

Solari cast Gina a grateful glance. "I'd be happy to put him up for the night, yes."

Rafael shook his head. "That would mean leaving his dad alone all night. I'm afraid Nat would be upset about that once he sobers up."

"Oh dear." Solari laid a hand on Nat's elbow. "Nat? Why don't you want to go home?"

To Rafael's shock, Nat's eyes welled with tears. He hung his head. "No reason. Jus' don't."

Instinct told Rafael the problem had nothing to do with illness or injury, but something much more painful. He stepped closer and took Nat's hands in his. "We can't stay out here on the sidewalk. Let me take you away from the bar, at least. Okay?"

Nat studied him through a curtain of fine blond hair. His gaze fell a little short of complete focus, telling Rafael exactly how drunk he was. "'Kay."

Relieved, Rafael slid an arm around Nat's waist. "C'mon, Wolfman. Let's go."

Nat leaned against him, one arm slung around his shoulders, his head resting on Rafael's. The trust implied in Nat's posture tugged at Rafael's heart. He hoped Nat still found him worthy of trust when he found out Rafael was taking him home after all.

Solari stood on tiptoe and kissed Nat's cheek. "Feel better, dear. I'll see you tomorrow. Or later today, I suppose, technically speaking."

Nat gave her a loopy grin. "I *totally* had a crush on you, b'fore Hollywood came 'long." He nuzzled Rafael's hair.

She blushed. "I know. Believe me, it would have been mutual if I were attracted to men."

Gina glowered, and Rafael stifled the urge to laugh. He couldn't help thinking of his own situation. Would Nat have ever even noticed him if the whole business with Solari hadn't happened first?

Solari squeezed Nat's free hand, then moved over to give Rafael a hug and a peck on the cheek. "Take care of him," she whispered. "I'm not sure what's wrong, exactly, but something's definitely bothering him. I'm worried."

Rafael nodded. "I'll look after him."

With a sad little smile, Solari drew away and followed Gina down the sidewalk toward the parking area. Rafael gathered Nat closer. "You ready to walk now?"

"Mm-hmm." Nat linked his hands around Rafael's neck and staggered along at his side. "You takin' me to your place t'fuck me? 'Cause that would be *aaawesome.*"

The mental image of bending Nat over the kitchen table and pounding into his ass burst like an exploding star across Rafael's vision. Damn, that was tempting. But he couldn't. Nat was too plastered to truly consent, never mind enjoy it.

"Maybe another time. When you're more likely to remember it." Rafael stumbled when Nat tripped and almost pulled them both down to the pavement. "Hang on to me. It's not far to my car."

Nat sighed, but allowed Rafael to lead him toward the car.

Alcohol apparently robbed Nat of his usual grace and made him grabby as hell. He slipped his fingers up Rafael's shirt and down his pants, and even managed to get his zipper halfway down before Rafael finally got him buckled into the car's passenger seat. With the job finally done, Rafael wiped sweat from his forehead as he skirted the front of the car to slide behind the wheel. He felt like he'd wrestled a multi-armed human noodle determined to molest him.

Nat's head lolled sideways when Rafael pulled out into the road. "Heeey."

"Hey, yourself." Rafael glanced at Nat. A confused crease dug between Nat's eyes. "You all right? You gonna be sick?"

"Uh-uh." Nat's hand flailed for a second, then latched on to Rafael's thigh with surprising strength. "I tol' Dad I found a man, but he didn't like that. Wanted me t'find a woman instead. Like I can jus' *do* that." His fingers clenched painfully tight on Rafael's leg. "I try so fucking hard. Why'm I never good enough?"

The walls Nat normally hid behind had crumbled, leaving years of built-up pain raw in his eyes and his low, mournful voice. Rafael's heart broke. He rested his hand over Nat's. "You're perfect the way you are. If your dad can't see that, then that's his problem."

A sweet, unguarded smile spread over Nat's face. "You're great."

"So are you." Rafael smiled back, thinking it was a good thing he already knew where Nat lived. He wasn't sure Nat remembered his own address right now.

Nat's eyelids drifted downward. "Where're we goin', Hollywood?"

Rafael steeled himself for the wrath of Nat. "I'm taking you home, Nat. You'll be pissed off at yourself later if you leave your dad alone all night. I'll stay with you if you want, but, yeah. I'm taking you home."

No answer. He glanced sideways and groaned.

Nat sat slumped against the seat, eyes shut and mouth slack, passed out cold.

Rafael sighed. If Nat actually remembered any of this later, he was going to be mortified.

The lights were still on inside the run-down little cottage on Fifth Street where Nat and his father lived. Rafael pulled his car into the short dirt drive behind Nat's truck and sat there for a moment, preparing himself for whatever the Horn family patriarch might have to say when some strange guy dragged his son in stinking drunk at almost two in the morning.

Nat stirred. "Mmph. Gotta pee."

"Okay." Rafael leaned over and pressed a kiss to Nat's damp brow. "Stay there. I'll come around and help you out of the car, okay?"

"'Kay."

Nat was struggling with the seat belt when Rafael opened the passenger-side door. Amused in spite of everything, Rafael ducked inside the car, reached across Nat's chest, and unbuckled the belt. "All right. Put your arms around my neck."

Nat obeyed, grinning in blatant flirtation. "Hey, hot stuff."

"Hey." Rafael laughed when Nat nuzzled his neck. "God, you're cute. Hang on."

Somewhat to his surprise, Nat did, his grip tight around Rafael's shoulders. Rafael slid his arms around Nat's waist, hauled him out of the car, and set him on his feet. Still hanging on, Rafael kicked the car door shut, then clicked the lock button on the key fob.

Keys. Shit.

"Nat? Where're your house keys?"

"Uh . . ." Frowning, Nat clung to Rafael with one hand and dug in the left front pocket of his jeans with the other. He came up empty, switched hands with exaggerated care, and fished his key ring out of the other front pocket, along with a crumpled receipt and a wad of lint. He handed the whole business to Rafael. "There."

"Thanks." Figuring he could work out which key was which once he got to the door, Rafael firmed his hold on Nat's swaying form and started up the walkway.

The second key Rafael tried turned out to be the house key. Which was good, because Nat had started to sag against his shoulder. He half carried Nat to the closest piece of furniture—an old but sturdy-looking armchair—and plopped him into it, then went back to shut the door.

Since he didn't know where Nat normally stored his keys, he put them on the small table beside the TV. When he turned around, Nat was watching him, eyes wide and solemn, his lower lip caught between his teeth.

"Didn't wanna come home," Nat mumbled, scratching his crotch. "Why'd you take me here?"

"Because you'd be mad at yourself tomorrow if you left your dad home alone all night."

Nat scowled. "Fuck 'im."

Rafael glance around. Three doors flanked the living area: two on one side, one on the other. One door led to a small bathroom, the other to what looked like a bedroom. The third was shut. Probably Mr. Horn's room, Rafael guessed. Which made the empty bedroom Nat's.

He crossed to the sofa and perched on the edge nearest Nat. "Look, you need to sleep off the booze. Then you'll realize I'm right." Nat *pffF*ed, and Rafael shook his head. He stood. "Come on, I'll help you to the bathroom. Then we'll get you ready for bed and I'll bring you some aspirin or something."

Nat let Rafael pull him to his feet. Face-to-face, Nat clutched Rafael close and stared into his eyes. "Stay with me. Please? Don't leave me alone."

He had no intention of doing any such thing. Especially since Nat's father apparently had a serious problem with Nat having a male lover.

Rafael laid a hand on Nat's flushed cheek and pressed a gentle kiss to Nat's lips. "Of course I'm staying."

Nat's smile could've lit up the blackest night. Rafael's heart lurched. Whatever happened in the morning, he'd face it. For Nat.

"Nat. Hey."

What. The fuck. Who was yelling? And why, Nat wondered, did he feel like someone had smacked him upside the head with a shovel, then shit in his mouth?

Groaning, Nat curled into a ball, hiding under his pillow. "Shut up and go away."

Soft laughter sounded behind him, muffled by foam and cotton. A warm body curled against his back, an arm snaking around his middle. "I know you feel like hell. Do you remember why?"

Wait. "Rafael?"

"Yep. You asked me to stay. As if I'd leave you alone." He kissed Nat's neck, sending pleasant shivers over his skin and chasing away some of the churning nausea. "You don't remember, do you?"

Disconnected flashes of last night played across the backs of Nat's eyelids: drinking at Ma Cougar's, arguing with some logger about something, getting punched in the face, Solari coaxing him outside. Or did he get thrown out? And, yeah, Rafael there on the sidewalk outside the bar, holding him up, putting him in the car, driving him home, even though Nat had very definitely said he hadn't wanted to go home.

Staying the night. Because Nat had asked him.

Interfering fucker. Nat couldn't decide whether to yell at him or thank him.

Moving carefully on account of the thumping agony in his skull, he laid his pillow aside and turned in Rafael's embrace. He opened his eyes just enough to see Rafael's face, bathed in the dull grayish light of an evidently rainy morning. "I remember enough. Sorry if I was an asshole."

"You weren't." Rafael bit his lip. "Sorry I took you home when you told me you didn't want to go."

Nat laughed, then stopped when pain shot through his skull. Fucking hangover. "No, you're not. I'd've been pissed off at myself if I hadn't come back home, so I guess I have to forgive you."

"Well, that's a relief." Rafael brushed the left side of his face with gentle fingers. "This is ugly. Anna's not gonna be happy about that. Neither is makeup."

Shit. "Yeah, well, I'm not happy about it either. Maybe we can start a club."

Rafael laughed, his eyes crinkling at the edges, and Nat couldn't help smiling in spite of how crappy he felt. Nobody ought to look as good first thing in the morning as Rafael did right now, with pillow creases on his cheek and his usually neat hair sticking up every which way.

The look in Rafael's eyes turned tender. He brushed the tangled hair away from Nat's face and kissed his forehead. "Stay right there, okay? I need to go back to my place and get ready for work, but I'm gonna go get you some water and something for your head before I leave."

Panic chased away enough of the pain to get Nat out of bed, even though he had to hang on to the bedside table to keep from passing out. "No, don't go out there alone. Dad might be up."

Rafael glanced at the closed bedroom door, then climbed out of bed. Both of them were wearing only their underwear. Damn, Nat had been out of it not to notice that before. Rafael came to him, wrapped both arms around him, and held him close, hands spread on his back. God, it felt *so good* to relax into Rafael's arms. Lean on Rafael's strength. Nat's eyes stung. He blinked until it went away.

"I'm not afraid of your father," Rafael murmured in Nat's ear. "If he loves you and wants you to be happy, he'll be glad I'm with you. And I can't believe he *wouldn't*. Let's give him a chance, okay?"

He was right. But Nat still felt bruised from his father's words last night. If he opened himself up and his dad stabbed him in the heart again, he didn't think he could take it.

He kept those thoughts to himself. "Doesn't mean you have to face him by yourself." Nat drew back, sat on the edge of the bed, and plucked last night's jeans off the floor. "We go out there together."

Thankfully, Rafael didn't argue. He nodded and started getting dressed.

When they went hand in hand into the living room, Nat's dad was sitting on the sofa with the TV on, the sound down low. Adrenaline shot through Nat's blood. It drained away when he realized his father was asleep.

Weak with relief, Nat led Rafael into the kitchen and plopped into the closest chair. "He must've had trouble sleeping," Nat whispered. "He'll get up and watch TV when he can't sleep." It worried Nat, because he hadn't seen his dad asleep on the couch since he'd started taking the new meds the ER doc had recommended. Hadn't he been sleeping better lately? Was his dad about to take another turn for the worse? Shit, he hoped not.

Rafael studied Nat for several long seconds, like he knew exactly what Nat was thinking. Then he turned without a word, took a glass from the cabinet, and filled it with tap water. "Here." He set the glass in front of Nat. "You need to hydrate. I'll get you some ibuprofen. You guys don't have any aspirin."

Nat didn't argue. He finished the water before Rafael got back from the bathroom. Rafael fetched him a refill. He swallowed the pills.

Smiling, Rafael raked a hand through Nat's hair. "You want me to fix you some breakfast?"

The idea of food made Nat's stomach try to climb up his throat. "No, thanks."

"You should eat a little something, so the ibuprofen won't upset your stomach." Rafael started opening cabinets and scanning the contents. "Here. Crackers." He grabbed a half-empty sleeve of saltines and set them on the table. "Eat a few, at least."

"Yeah, okay." Nat grabbed Rafael's hand and planted a kiss on the inside of his wrist. "Thanks. For everything."

A sweet warmth shone in Rafael's eyes, making Nat's pulse race. "Sure. I'm glad I could help."

For a long moment Nat couldn't look away from Rafael's face, reflecting his own heart back at him. He pushed to his feet and leaned close to whisper in Rafael's ear. "Better get out while the getting's good. I don't have to be in till this afternoon. I'll see you then."

Rafael glanced toward the couch, where Nat's dad was grumbling in his sleep. "Text me when you get in." He planted a closed-mouthed kiss on Nat's lips, fingers toying with his hair like always. "I'll see you later." He started to say something else, stopped, and smiled. "Yeah. See you."

Nat watched him leave, then slumped back into the old chair, one hand planted over the hard, tight warmth in his chest.

CHAPTER TWELVE

"Cut," said Rafael. "That's a wrap." He glanced at Anna, who gave him a double thumbs-up. He grinned. "Great job, everybody. Thank you."

The set erupted into the usual post-shoot whirl of activity. Heart hammering with nerves and elation, Rafael turned to face Anna. "Well? What do you think?"

"I think you did incredibly well. There are a few things I would've done differently, but I don't think that's anything you need to worry about. Every director has their own style. Yours isn't the same as mine, and that's fine." Smiling, she squeezed his shoulder. "I like what I'm seeing here, Rafael. In fact, I'd love for you to direct an entire episode at some point. If you're up for it."

"Up for it?" He laughed, not even caring that he sounded positively giddy. "Hell yes, I'm up for it. Just tell me when."

"Well, it'll have to wait a little while. Everything's planned out for the next few months. But I have something in mind." She hooked her arm through his elbow and led him toward the exit. "Come on. Let's go get a coffee and we'll talk about it."

Rafael floated along beside her, grinning like an idiot because he couldn't help it. Over the last couple of weeks he'd finally started working alongside Anna in an apprentice role, and it was pure heaven. Not only did she appreciate his previous work, she had a sharp eye for how to utilize his particular talents on *Wolf's Landing*. His first try at directing a scene on his own today had gone better than he'd dreamed. And now it looked like he had a real shot at a career. All thanks to Anna.

"I can't thank you enough for this chance," he said as they took their flat whites and went to find a spot to sit. "I mean, getting to direct an episode of *Wolf's Landing*? It's a dream come true for me. I can't believe this is my *life* right now."

Laughing, Anna pulled out a plastic chair at a miraculously empty two-person table and sank into it. "I hope you still feel that way when you're on the twentieth take of the first scene and wondering if you can manage to get it all done in the time you've given yourself." She pointed her almond biscotti at him. "Which, by the way, is never enough. But you make it work. And that, my child, is the bitter yet addictive essence of TV directing."

Rafael snickered into his cup. "I can see that. Nothing like successfully conquering a challenge to make you want to keep doing it."

"Exactly." Anna's phone chirped. She pulled it out of her pocket. Her expression turned stormy when she saw whatever was on the screen. "Oh hell. Not again."

"What is it?" Belatedly realizing maybe it was none of his business, Rafael backpedaled. "I mean, you don't have to tell me, obviously. I was just curious."

"No, it's not a secret or anything. Would be better if it was, actually." She held her phone out to him. "Look."

He took the phone, dread sitting like a boulder in his stomach. The online chatter since Solari had come out hadn't always been kind, to put it mildly. Solari had put on a brave face for the public, but privately the ugliness was getting to her. If the trolls and haters had ramped it up . . .

And, yeah, they had. #GayLanding was the number three trending topic on Twitter, and while the show's supporters were doing their best, right now the hashtag dripped disgust, disdain, and a frightening level of hostility, mostly leveled at Solari.

Another dyke on #GayLanding. Are normal people out of style now? Disgusting.

Bitch need da D. Fuck out da lesbo.

Burn in hell, moslum cunt

Who got vid of Alecia & her gf, I pay cash $$.

Feeling sick, Rafael handed Anna's phone back to her. "Jesus."

"Yeah." Anna gulped coffee, her gaze focused on nothing. "I know she must've seen it. This crap's been going on ever since the press conference, but it's gotten a lot worse in the last couple of days.

And I'm afraid it's going to get her in trouble with Finn, which could be bad."

As in losing-her-job bad, Rafael knew. Anna's co-executive producer wasn't the nicest guy in the world, and he didn't like it when his stars' personal lives caused bad publicity.

Rafael's phone meowed on the table beside him. A quick glance showed an incoming text from Solari. "Speaking of which, that's her. She wants me to bring her a chai and some yogurt before she has to be on set."

Anna's eyebrows pulled together. "She didn't say anything about the Twitter business?"

"Nope. But she wouldn't say anything in a text."

"No, I guess not."

He pushed his chair back and stood. "Could we get together another time and talk about your ideas for an episode for me to direct?"

She nodded. "I'll email you with the details. Let me know if Solari needs me, okay?"

"Sure thing. Thanks, Anna."

He headed back toward the coffee bar as Anna's phone rang. It was a minor miracle she'd gone this long without anyone calling her, actually. Too bad they hadn't gotten around to discussing her thoughts about the episode she wanted him to direct.

Me. Directing an episode of Wolf's Landing. *Holy shit.* It was no exaggeration to say that such a thing could launch his career.

An electric thrill ran through his bones. He couldn't wait to tell Nat. He'd been even more quiet and reserved than usual ever since the fight with his dad. If Rafael's news could make Nat smile again, even for a moment, he'd call it a victory.

He fetched Solari's chai and a nonfat, sugar-free lemon Greek yogurt—her favorite—and hurried off to her trailer. A couple of burly security guards paced the perimeter, put in place by Anna since things had started getting nasty online. Both of them knew Rafael on sight at this point. The one currently on the door side—Vaughn—let him by with a quick nod. Man of few words, that one.

Rafael climbed the steps and knocked. "Solari? It's me, I have your tea and yogurt."

"Oh good. Come in."

Her voice sounded stuffy. Worried, Rafael opened the door and shut it quickly behind him, in case anyone outside had a zoom lens or something. One look at Solari's face told him she'd been crying. And he figured he knew why.

"Oh, honey." He crossed the small room, set the cardboard tray on the table, and sat on the sofa beside Solari. Her knees were drawn up to her chest, and tears leaked from her red, swollen eyes. Heart breaking for her, he pulled her into a hug. "Don't listen to all those jerks. People are ignorant and mean, especially when they're jealous and unhappy. Everyone who knows you loves you. Never forget that."

She laughed, the sound needle sharp. "I know. And I'm grateful, believe me. But sometimes it's simply not enough."

Oh crap. This wasn't about any online bullshit.

Rafael sat back enough to study her face. "What happened?"

"Gina had to fly back to LA late last night. And of course I knew she would need to return to work at some point. I would never hold that against her." Solari's lips curved into a sad smile. "She was so relieved to be going back home. She tried to hide it, but I could tell. And the thing is, I can't blame her. I'm used to living in a fishbowl. She isn't. And the stress of it has already put such a distance between us, Rafael. That's the worst part. It used to be that whenever we were actually together, we were fine. We were *good*. But ever since that press conference, we've fought constantly, over nothing at all." She sighed. Rubbed at her swollen eyes with one hand. "This is exactly what I was afraid would happen."

"I'm so sorry. What can I do to help? Anything you need, anytime, let me know." He took her hand in both of his. "You know Nat and I are here for you, right? We love you."

She gave him a watery smile. "I know. I love you both as well, and I'm so very grateful for your friendship." She squeezed his fingers. "How is Nat? He's seemed so preoccupied lately, ever since that night at Ma Cougar's. I've been worried about him."

What to tell her? If Nat hadn't said anything, Rafael didn't think he should. "There's some tension between Nat and his dad," he hedged. "Plus you know his dad has some health problems. All that's kind of weighing him down."

"Oh. I see." Her dark eyes shone with sympathy. "I'm so glad he has you, Rafael. He keeps everyone else at arm's length, even his friends. But I think you and he have become quite close, and I think that's good for you both."

Warmth flooded Rafael's veins, like it did every time he thought of Nat. "I know it's been awesome for me. I like to think it's been good for Nat too. I hope so. He's become very important to me."

A smile brightened her face, chasing away some of the sadness. "I'm so happy to hear that. For what it's worth, I do believe that you've become important to him as well."

Rafael's heart turned over. He wasn't ready to put a name to his feelings for Nat. He only knew that it was something deeper than friendship. "I came out here for my career. For the chance to maybe work with Anna. And that's happening, which is awesome. Better than I'd ever dreamed. But I never expected to find someone like Nat. I mean, we're still new, but it feels *right*. You know? And I didn't expect that."

"Oh, my darling." Solari framed his face in her palms and pulled his head down, resting their foreheads together. "Life's surprises can be beautiful, or terrible. Learn to cherish the good ones."

He clung to her small, steady hands. She was right. His relationship with Nat wasn't something he'd planned. But it was good. It made him happy. *Nat* made him happy. And maybe it was time they talked about the future. How to keep going when the day inevitably came that Rafael had to go back to Hollywood. Because as much as he loved it here, he didn't intend to spend his whole life as a PA. He had bigger plans for his future.

Tomorrow, he promised himself. *I'll talk to him tomorrow.*

At least, that was Rafael's plan. Life, however, had a way of screwing things up. Between his duties with Solari and his part-time apprenticeship with Anna, Rafael was run off his feet, and Nat's filming schedule had exploded lately. Meaning they hadn't spent as much time together as either of them would've liked.

In fact, a whole week passed between Rafael's vow to discuss their future with Nat and the next time they were able to spend more than a few minutes alone.

It was a warm, sunny Saturday in early May, the kind of day that drew even the most diehard couch potato outdoors to enjoy the flower-scented breeze and the sparkle of sunshine on the water. Rafael had suggested a hike up to the same hilltop where Nat had taken him before, and Nat had readily agreed.

This time, Rafael insisted on carrying the backpack with the food in it. Which kept getting him narrow-eyed glances from Nat. "Seriously, Hollywood. You should let me carry that." Nat helped him scramble over a huge tree that had fallen across the forest path. "It looks heavy."

"Well, it's not." Rafael answered Nat's raised eyebrows with a defiant glare. "I'm not a complete weakling, you know. I can carry a backpack."

A slow smile spread over Nat's face. "Uh-huh. You don't want me to know what's in there."

Damn. Busted. He'd brought wine, homemade empanadas, and decadent chocolate tarts from Cookie Crumbles. A strange but special meal to complement the speech he'd been practicing in his head for the past few days.

Not that he was going to *admit* that.

He lifted his chin and did his best to convey the sense of looking down at Nat in spite of being several inches shorter. "Maybe I want to prove to a certain werewolf I know that I'm more than a pretty Hollywood face."

The teasing gleam in Nat's pale eyes softened into a fondness that made Rafael's heart thump. Nat sidled closer, slipped his arms around Rafael's waist, and pressed against him. "You're way more than that."

Joy blossomed in Rafael's chest, stealing his breath. Framing Nat's face with his hands, he tilted his head for a kiss. And it felt like a dream, like a fairy tale, kissing in the brilliant green forest, no one around but the two of them, the sun breaking through the branches in fitful bursts and birdsong ringing in the air around them. Rafael wondered if they'd fallen into their own time bubble, drifting along forever in this one perfect moment.

Nat broke the kiss and trailed his lips down Rafael's throat. "I hope you brought supplies."

"Supplies?" Shivers raced over Rafael's skin when Nat nibbled the sensitive spot where his neck curved into his shoulder. "Mmm. Do that again."

Nat obliged, biting hard enough to tear a gasp from Rafael. "C'mon, don't play dumb. You know. *Supplies.*"

When he got it, the knowledge of what Nat wanted to do on the hilltop sent all the blood rushing from Rafael's brain to his crotch. "Oh. *Supplies.*" He clung to Nat, head spinning. "Um . . ."

"That means no, doesn't it?"

Rafael's cheeks heated. "Well, honestly, public sex never occurred to me."

Nat laughed, his breath warm and soft on Rafael's neck. "I don't know if you could really call it *public.* It's pretty unlikely anyone else'll be up there."

"True. Still . . ."

"Still, we can consider this me popping your public sex cherry?" Nat lifted his head and grinned.

Rafael snickered. "Whatever makes you happy, Wolfman." He caught a stray strand of Nat's baby-fine hair and gave it a tug. "Let's get going. Now that you brought up the possibility of getting some action, I want to hustle on up there."

Heat chased away the amusement in Nat's eyes. "Who says we have to wait? Maybe we can't fuck, but I can sure as shit imagine you sitting on that log there while I suck your dick."

The mental image hit Rafael like a runaway train. His knees wobbled. "You have a hell of a way with words."

"'Cause I like to use my mouth." Nat sank to his knees, slowly, his gaze holding Rafael's the whole time. "What d'you say, Hollywood? You want me to suck your cock? Right here in the woods?" He lowered his head. Buried his face in Rafael's crotch and breathed deep. "Mmm. Smells like you want me to."

Oh God. Rafael threaded his fingers through Nat's hair. His pulse thudded in his ears. "I could totally go for that right now, actually."

"First things first." Grinning like the wolf-demon he was, Nat rose gracefully to his feet and started pulling off his clothes.

For Nat, watching Rafael watch him undress was a huge turn-on. The way Rafael's round cheeks flushed, the way he sucked on his plump lower lip and stared at Nat's too-thin chest with unfiltered lust smoldering in those dark eyes . . .

"I like how you look at me." Nat tossed aside his T-shirt and toed off his shoes. He lifted his feet one at a time to take off his socks, enjoying the feel of the cool leaf litter on his bare soles. "Like you want to eat me up."

"You could say that." Rafael let out a shaky breath when Nat wriggled out of his jeans and underwear and stood naked on the damp forest floor, his balls drawn up tight and his prick so hard it ached. "I'd love to lick you all over right now."

Oh, hell yeah. "I'll allow it. After I make you come."

Rafael's eyelids fluttered. "Ah."

God, Nat loved that helpless little sound. Loved that he had the power to turn Rafael silent with desire. He'd never been able to do that before. Not with any of the few casual sex partners he'd had, or the girl he'd thought he was in love with back in high school. Not even with Lem, who'd been a great lay, and—for a little while—a friend.

For the first time in his life, he felt good in his own skin, and he liked it.

His gaze still locked with Rafael's, he stepped forward until their bodies almost touched. He could see the rapid pulse throbbing in Rafael's throat. Lust and something else—something sweeter, something that Nat couldn't bring himself to name directly, even in his own mind—shone in Rafael's eyes. Rafael reached out to rest his palms on Nat's hips. His hands shook, and Nat fell a little bit harder.

Chest tight, Nat ran his hands over Rafael's shoulders, caressing the strong, hard, streamlined muscle under Rafael's shirt. He grasped the backpack straps, lifted, and eased them down Rafael's arms, smiling at Rafael's unresisting compliance. Turned-on Rafael was as adorable as he was sexy.

The backpack went *clink* when it dropped into the leaves. Nat spared half a second to wonder what in the hell Rafael had in there, but he couldn't be bothered to think about it for too long. He had more interesting things on his mind. Like getting his mouth around Rafael's delicious dick.

He sank to his knees like he'd done a few minutes ago. Rafael's cheeks flushed red under the sparse stubble Nat found so charming. His fingers found their usual spot in Nat's hair, his eyes drifting shut when Nat pushed his shirt up and nuzzled his belly. "God, Nat."

"Mmm." Nat drew a deep breath spiced with skin, soap, sweat, and a hint of woodsy cologne. And over it all, the heady, drugging scent of Rafael's arousal. "You smell good."

Rafael's eyes opened. He peered down at Nat with lust and tenderness battling for territory on his face. His lips quirked into a wicked smile. "You look good kneeling at my feet like that."

The quaver in Rafael's voice—like he was barely keeping himself together—did all kinds of interesting things to Nat's insides. Grinning, he flipped open the button on Rafael's jeans and tugged down the zipper. "Hold on to your socks, little boy. The big, bad Wolfman's gonna eat you up."

Rafael's mouth opened. Whatever he might've said dissolved into a breathy *aaahhh* when Nat yanked his pants and underwear down over his hips and swallowed his cock in one smooth move.

In the past, Nat had never been the one to take the lead in sex. Too much trouble for too little reward. Now, with Rafael, he found he liked being the aggressor. Liked the way Rafael moaned his name, the way he trembled and pulled Nat's hair every time he deep-throated Rafael's prick.

It felt good. It felt *powerful*, counterintuitive as that sounded when he was kneeling naked in the dirt and Rafael stood above him still mostly clothed. But he couldn't deny it. He tasted sweet surrender when Rafael shot down his throat with an echoing cry, and he knew he'd crave that feeling every day for the rest of his life.

He swallowed, again and again. Somewhere in the distance, he heard a mechanical trill. Nat's sex-fogged brain decided to ignore it, and it quit after a few seconds. Rafael's hips stopped moving too, and his dick started to go soft. He drew back to study Rafael's face.

His cheeks were pink, his eyes heavy-lidded and glazed, and Nat's heart turned over.

Wrapping his arms around Rafael's hips, he rested his cheek on Rafael's flat belly. "You taste so fucking good."

"Mmm." Rafael unclenched his fists from Nat's hair and petted his head in long, soothing strokes. "Do I get to taste *you* now?"

The mental image nearly made Nat come all by itself, he was so on edge. "You bet your cute little butt you do."

Rafael laughed. "Lie down on that fallen tree, and spread your legs."

Oh, damn. Pulse racing, Nat hurried to do what Rafael said. He sat on the enormous tree trunk, then lowered himself carefully onto his back. The wood was damp and a little cold, but the heavy growth of moss kept it soft and protected him from splinters. And it was as wide as a sofa. All in all, not a bad bed.

He hooked his hands under his knees, pulling them up to his chest and opening his thighs wide. "Come and get me, Hollywood."

And there went that sweet blush again, coloring Rafael's cheeks hot pink and clashing adorably with the sinful promise glittering in his eyes. Grinning like a demon, Rafael stalked forward, hiked up his pants, and planted himself on the fallen tree between Nat's legs. He ran his hands up the insides of Nat's thighs, then back down again, until his thumbs brushed the underside of Nat's balls.

Nat drew in a hissing breath through his teeth. "Jesus. Stop teasing and touch me already."

One neatly groomed brow lifted. "Like this?" Rafael curled his fingers around Nat's shaft, bent, and licked a wet stripe across the head of his cock.

Goddamn if that didn't blast all the words right out of Nat's brain. "Uhhh," he moaned, one hand hanging on to his leg for dear life and the other groping for any part of Rafael he could reach. His fingers skated through Rafael's too-short-to-grab hair, clipped his ear, and ended up grasping at empty air.

Rafael, evil creature that he was, laughed. "Try not to kick me when you come, Wolfman."

A tiny corner of Nat's mind argued, silently, that he'd never kicked anyone during sex in his life, and why did Rafael think he'd start now? But the protest died before it got a good foothold, on account of Rafael's lips sliding down his cock, all the way to the root, throat squeezing the head in a way that had Nat seeing stars.

When Rafael pulled off long enough to slick a couple of fingers with spit and push them up Nat's ass, Nat gasped and flung his feet into the air. *Good thing Rafael's down there instead of up here fucking me, or he really* would *have gotten kicked.* Nat let out a laugh that morphed into a keening cry when Rafael's clever fingers nailed his gland. "Oh, oh fuck. Fuck."

Rafael *hmm*ed with his mouth full, his throat vibrating around Nat's prick, and that did it. Nat came so hard his vision sparkled at the edges, his hands digging into his thighs—*no kicking*—and soft little *uh-uh-uh* noises bleeding from his mouth.

The orgasm shook him, wrung him out, and left him sprawled limp and sated on the dead tree. He blinked blearily at the green canopy overhead while Rafael lapped up the last splatters of semen like it was ice cream or something. Nat giggled. Fucking *giggled.* Which was so wrong it made him giggle even more.

Rafael lifted his head, amusement curving his lips—all red and swollen from *sucking Nat's cock*, Jesus—into a crooked smile. "What's so funny?"

"You. Me. Us, here." Nat swooped one arm in an arc overhead, indicating the forest and the current situation in general. "I dunno. I think maybe coming makes me get silly."

Chuckling, Rafael took Nat's hands in his and tugged until he sat up. "Silly Nat is cute. I like it." He peered at Nat with vulnerability shining in his eyes. "I like that you feel that comfortable with me. I know you don't let everybody that close, and, well, I like being the person you let in."

Something sharp and sweet spiked through Nat's chest. Because words had never been easy for him, he draped his legs over Rafael's, wound both arms around Rafael's neck, and kissed him. *You're important to me*, he said with the press of his lips and tongue. *No one else has ever been this close.*

Rafael's right hand spread between Nat's shoulder blades, the left cupping his skull like he was something infinitely precious, and Nat thought maybe he'd gotten his point across.

A muffled *brring* cut the quiet. This time, without the urgency of sex clouding his head, Nat allowed himself to recognize his cell phone. Apparently they weren't quite out of range here.

Nat broke the kiss. "I should answer that."

"Definitely." Rafael touched Nat's cheek and flashed a wide, bright smile as he reached for the pile of clothes he'd left on the forest floor.

Nat's answering smile died when he saw the name that popped up on his phone's screen. He swiped it on with suddenly clumsy fingers, his pulse whooshing in his ears. "Mrs. Hawk?"

"Nat. Thank God." Her usually calm voice had a panicked edge, and Nat's stomach knotted. "Where are you?"

"I'm . . . hiking. With a friend." He glanced at Rafael. A worried crease dug between his brown eyes. He mouthed, *What's wrong?* Nat shook his head. "What's going on? What happened?"

"It's your dad, Nat. There was an accident. He's on his way to the hospital in Port Angeles right now. You need to get over there. It's bad."

Numbness spread from Nat's core through his body, paralyzing him. "What happened?"

"There was a fire. I guess your dad fell asleep. I saw smoke coming out around the edge of the kitchen door and called 911, and, well." She drew a wobbly breath. Blew it out. "He's alive. But he's not good."

Oh God. Nat ran a shaking hand through his hair. "Where was the sitter?"

"Sitter?" She sounded confused. "No one else was there."

Shit. Shit, shit, shit. His dad must've sent another one home. Nat's throat constricted.

Mrs. Hawk was talking again. "Nat, honey, you get on over to the hospital, okay?"

"Yeah. I will. Thank you." He ended the call and sat there, staring at nothing, feeling bruised inside.

"Nat?" Rafael cupped his face in both hands, studying him with concern. "What's going on?"

"That was Mrs. Hawk, my neighbor. She said there was a fire at my house, and they took my dad to the hospital." Nat heard his own voice as if from a great distance. "He must've sent his sitter home again. Why does he keep *doing* that?"

"Oh my God, Nat."

He stood, letting Rafael's hands fall away from him. "I have to get dressed. Sorry. I didn't mean to ruin our picnic."

Rafael's eyes widened. "What? God, no, that's . . . Don't even worry about that." He jumped off the log, picked up Nat's T-shirt, and shook leaves off it while Nat stepped into his underwear. "I'll drive you, okay? You shouldn't be alone right now."

His first instinct was to protest. But he really, *really* didn't want to face whatever was about to happen by himself. "That'd be great. Thanks." He pulled on his jeans, zipped and buttoned them on autopilot, then took his shirt from Rafael and slipped it over his head.

For whatever reason, the reality of what was happening didn't hit until he'd finished lacing his shoes. Then it slammed into him like a truck. He grasped Rafael's hand and fought back the terror squeezing his lungs. "Mrs. Hawk said it was bad, Rafael. What if . . . What if . . ."

He couldn't say it. But Rafael understood, because he was that sort of guy. He wove his fingers through Nat's, steadied Nat's body with an arm around his waist, anchored his mind with a calm, unwavering presence. "Don't. Let's see what the situation is first. Okay?" He kissed Nat, soft and sweet, easing some of his fear. "I'm with you, whatever happens. Remember that. You don't have to do any of this alone."

Tears stung the backs of Nat's eyes, but didn't fall. He nodded, his throat too tight to speak. Rafael grabbed the backpack and slung it onto his shoulder, and the two of them took off back down the slope as fast as they could manage through the thick undergrowth.

They'd almost reached the trailhead before Nat thought to check the call he'd ignored while he'd been blissed out sucking Rafael's cock. Dread churning in his gut, he thumbed on his phone and checked his call log. And stopped in his tracks, fighting the urge to drop to the ground and curl into a guilty ball.

The call he hadn't answered was from his father.

CHAPTER THIRTEEN

The next couple of hours of Nat's life passed in snapshots. Green leaves, birds chattering, thunder, a brief, cold squall, Rafael taking his truck keys and driving him to Port Angeles. Surprise that Hollywood drove a stick. Fierce gratitude that he did.

The police called on the way to the hospital. They wanted to talk to him. The feeling was not mutual, and Nat said so in no uncertain terms. What could they tell him that he needed to know right now? And he sure as shit didn't have any information that would help them.

And here Nat still was, who the fuck knew how long after. A couple of days, he figured, or near enough, going by the nursing shift changes, the number of doctor visits, and the fact that Rafael had gone away, come back, and gone away again since the whole ugly business started.

Yawning, Nat rose from the recliner at his father's bedside, stretched, and rubbed the grit from his eyes. The glass-enclosed cubicle was dim, the only light coming from the machines: IV, ventilator, the lights on the hospital bed. A curtain across the door blocked the brightness of the nurse's station.

Somewhere beyond this little room, an alarm chimed. It was answered by running feet, voices, more light. People taking care of business. Yanking some flagging life back from the brink, maybe.

Don't think about it. Just don't.

He rested his elbows on the hospital bed's side rail and watched his dad's face, like he'd done for however long he'd been here. His father looked old, skin gray and crepey, colorless lips slack around the plastic tube snaking into his lungs, hooked up to the ventilator that kept him alive.

His eyes didn't move under the lids threaded with tiny blue veins. He didn't make his usual fearful little noises, and his arms and legs didn't jerk like they normally did when he slept.

No restless dreams for Jerome Horn. Not anymore.

Pain, fury, and guilt swelled in Nat's gut, the way it had over and over since he'd first arrived in this little glass cubicle. He curled forward, head in his hands, fighting the tears he refused to let fall. Rafael had told him not to give up, and he would damn well *not* give up. Not as long as his father kept breathing.

Well. As long as that fucking machine kept breathing *for* him.

And how long are you gonna let that keep happening, Nat? Huh? How long are you gonna keep him alive, because you'll feel like it'll be your fault if he dies?

"Shut up," he whispered to the increasingly loud voice in the back of his head. He knew his dad's wishes. Better than anyone, since his uncle and his sister had long ago washed their lily-white hands of any responsibility for the family's resident addict. And for all his self-destructive tendencies, for all the shit he'd been through in the last few years, Nat's father had never lost his unquenchable desire to live. Nat wasn't going to be the person to decide his dad could not, should not, or somehow wouldn't *want* to live anymore, simply because he'd accidentally overdosed.

It *had* been an accident. Nat wasn't sure of much in his life anymore, but he had zero doubt about that. The voice mail his dad had left that day was short and vague, but the meaning became obvious in the glaring light of hindsight. *"I left the pan on the stove, Nat. It's smoking. But I'm so sleepy. Can't move."*

Nat closed his eyes, remembering the sound of his father's rough, labored breathing, followed by those last, slurred words that would haunt him for the rest of his days. *"Think I took too many pills. 'M scared."* Then a clunk, and silence for another minute and a half until the phone cut the message off.

The fire fighters who'd managed to save his house—the only damage was the burnt stove and one scorched kitchen wall—had found the Robaxin bottle on the coffee table, next to a whole six-pack of empty beer cans. Judging by the number of pills left versus how many *ought* to be left, the doc thought Nat's dad must've taken at least six or seven at once. Maybe more. And probably triple the prescribed dose of the tramadol Dr. Takoda had given him to replace the Vicodin. That plus the booze had been too much for his system to handle on top of the smoke inhalation. If Mrs. Hawk hadn't spotted the smoke coming from the half-open kitchen window and kicked in the back door . . .

Christ.

Opening his eyes, Nat straightened up and paced to the window. It was four in the morning, according to the clock readout on the heart monitor. The streets of Port Angeles were deserted except for the occasional car slicing through the rain. Droplets glittered in the streetlight glow. The view mirrored how Nat felt: lonely, gloomy, empty. Hopeless, no matter how hard he tried to believe everything would turn out okay.

His phone buzzed in his back pocket, startling him. He pulled it out and rolled his eyes when he saw the text from his sister, asking how their dad was doing. Anger twisted his insides. She'd flat-out refused to fly to Washington to visit her comatose, critically ill father. Why in the hell was she pretending to be interested now?

Fuming, Nat stabbed at her tiny picture and hit the phone icon. She answered on the second ring. "Nat? I didn't figure you'd be up yet."

Why'd you text me at 4 a.m. then? "Dad hasn't woken up. The doctor doesn't think he ever will. Everybody here's trying to talk me into taking him off life support and letting him die."

When he paused, the familiar pain kicking him in the lungs, she jumped in. "I'm sorry, Nat. I know this must be hard for you."

It was all Nat could do not to scream at her. The only thing that kept his voice low was knowing for a solid fact that he'd get thrown out of the ICU if he lost control. And he would *not* let that happen.

"You don't know *shit*." He paced the tile floor, trying to burn off some of the rage boiling inside him. "You haven't laid eyes on either of us in *thirteen fucking years.* Not even after Dad's accident. No, you couldn't be bothered to help out. Too damn busy with your fucking *shop* and Colin's fucking *art.*" He put air quotes around the word with his free hand, never mind that Abby couldn't see it. "Meanwhile, guess who was back here in that shitty old house, watching Dad waste away and turn into a fucking pill addict? Me, that's who. Because you were too fucking selfish to ever help, even a little bit. And now you're gonna fucking *text* me to ask how he is?" He snorted. "Please. Don't pretend you give a shit."

Abby was silent so long he thought she'd set her phone down and walked away. He was about to ask if she was still there when she spoke again, her voice low and cold. "Dad treated me like crap my whole life. You know that. Mom too. She always defended him, but I saw how he talked to her. Like she was less than him. Like everything she had or did was by his leave, you know? She used to work, d'you remember? She was a bank executive. And he guilted her into quitting because she made more money than him."

Nat swallowed nausea. "I don't remember any of that."

"I figured. You were only six when she left the bank. And you were always Dad's favorite. His *son*." She sighed. Her voice softened, turning sad. "And you know how Dad was after Mom died. Acting like it was my duty to stay in Bluewater Bay and take care of the family. Like what *I* wanted didn't even matter. I couldn't stay, Nat."

"Yeah, I know." Nat dropped into the recliner. "I get it. I do. But can't you at least put all that aside long enough to fly out here and help me deal with this?"

She went quiet. Nat clenched his free hand in his lap. *Come on. Don't make me face this by myself.*

"I can't," she said, barely audible over the constant noise of the machines keeping their father alive. "Even if I could afford the plane ticket and the time away from work, which isn't a sure thing at all, I don't think I can stand to look at him again. He's been out of my life for a long time, and I want to keep it that way."

"Even if he dies? Even if you never get another chance to reconcile?" Nat struggled to get the words out past the aching tightness in his throat. "C'mon, Abby."

"I don't want to reconcile with him. And I don't care if he dies."

Nat flinched at her harsh words and harsher tone. Leaning forward, he rubbed at the dull pain in his chest. He wanted to beg her to help him. To not leave him to handle their father's death alone like he'd had to handle everything else since the logging accident. Maybe a little guilt would change her mind.

He bit back the *please please please* poised and ready to fly. The last thing he wanted, or needed, was help given under duress. Especially from his sister.

"Fine." *That* word, he had to force out through his teeth. "I'll text you when he dies. Maybe you can have a party."

He cut off the call before she could answer. Whatever she might say, he didn't want to hear it.

Restless, he stood and wandered over to the window again, his phone in his hand. The need to talk to Rafael was a near-physical ache, but he couldn't call. Not yet. Rafael wouldn't be awake for another hour or so. Normally he wouldn't be up *that* early, but Solari had to be in the makeup chair at six this morning, which meant Rafael would be there with her. Even so, Nat knew he shouldn't be calling Raphael at work.

A dark part of Nat hated *Wolf's Landing* and everyone involved in it for keeping Rafael away from him right now. Why, wondered the bruised and bitter corner of Nat's psyche, was he always the one getting the short end of the stick? Why was he never allowed to have what he needed?

His sensible side reminded him that Rafael had to work, and so did Solari. That Anna had generously given him as much time off as she could manage with the shooting schedule, meaning he could be with his father for another week at least without worrying about losing his job. And the Hawks had offered to look after the house, letting the fire investigators and police in when necessary.

In fact, Nat was damn lucky, and he knew it. Maybe he ought to remind himself of that more often.

Behind him, one of the machines attached to his dad went *bong . . . bong . . . bong*. Nat turned, heart in his throat like every time one of the alarms sounded. A readout on the monitor had turned red. He frowned, trying to figure out what it meant, but it was all Greek to him.

The cubicle door opened and the nurse—Tara?—swept in, full of calm efficiency. She smiled at Nat as she flipped on the light. "Hi, Nat. Couldn't sleep?"

He didn't bother to answer that. Could *anyone* sleep in the ICU? At least they'd let him stay. "What's wrong? Why's the alarm going off?"

"It's his blood pressure. It's dropped below the lower limit we set again." She examined Nat's father quickly but thoroughly, going through the routine Nat had watched dozens of times but still didn't really understand. "We'll titrate up his Levophed. That ought to help."

Nat didn't know much about any of the drugs they'd been pumping into his dad. But he'd figured out that this particular one was supposed to keep a person's blood pressure up when the body couldn't manage on its own. Tara and the other nurses had been in here more than once to turn up the dose on that and the other meds meant to keep his dad's blood pressure from bottoming out. And still, it kept dropping, and they kept titrating up, as they called it.

That could only mean one thing: the drugs weren't working. Nat's father was going to die. It wasn't simply a taunt to make Abby feel guilty. Jerome Horn's life was going to end here in this sterile glass box, in a city where no one knew him, his wasted body bristling with lines and tubes and nobody but his disappointment of a son to mourn him.

The enormity of his father's existence, erased and forgotten by everyone but him, froze Nat to his bones. How had it come to this? For a second, Nat imagined himself staring down a tunnel into the past, seeing Jerome Horn as he'd once been: strong, vital, *alive*. A good father, in spite of his flaws. What had happened to that man? How had he become this frail shell lying in the ICU bed? And how was Nat supposed to let him go?

Numb, he watched Tara fiddle with the IV pump, study vital sign readouts, examine his dad again, and finally leave the room when she was satisfied that her patient wasn't going to die right that minute. He thought she asked him if he needed a cup of coffee or anything, and he was sure he shook his head and said something in answer, but the whole thing felt remote. Distant. Like a show playing on a TV in the next room with the sound turned off.

Tara flipped off the overhead light on her way out. Alone in the dimness with the relentless machines and his dying father, Nat went to the window again to watch the rain.

He was still alone fourteen hours and twenty-two minutes later when his father died.

Because he'd refused to sign the Do Not Resuscitate forms—*Dad never would've agreed to that, I know it*—they had to go through a

Code Blue first. All the alarms pinged at once, and even Nat could tell that the heart monitor's readout looked wrong, an irregular wavy line instead of the usual spiky repeating pattern. A whole crowd of nurses and doctors busted into the room, kicked him out, and started working over his dad with calm urgency.

The still-numb, detached part of Nat wished Rafael could be here to film the scene. The way the group worked together was impressive. *Way* better than any TV show or movie he'd ever seen.

The part of Nat watching his father slip away right in front of him wished Rafael could be here to hold him together.

When a doctor he'd never laid eyes on before emerged from the controlled chaos in the cubicle with a solemn sadness on her face, Nat knew what she was going to say before she got close enough to speak to him. "He's dead, isn't he?"

Surprisingly, his voice didn't shake or anything. He must be a better actor than he'd thought, because inside he was screaming.

The doctor nodded, her gaze holding his. "Yes. I'm so sorry." She reached out and brushed her fingertips over his arm. "We'll have some paperwork for you to sign in a few minutes. Is there anyone we can call for you?"

He shook his head. "No, thanks. I'll do it."

"Okay." She watched him for a few seconds with the doctor-stare he'd gotten way too familiar with over the past few years. "Again, I'm very sorry for your loss. Please let us know if there's anything at all we can do for you."

He nodded and dredged up a smile as she turned and strode away to do whatever doctors did when they weren't trying to save patients. The day nurse—Nat couldn't remember his name—came out of the cubicle after a couple of minutes and rested one big, square hand on Nat's shoulder. "Nat. I'm really sorry, man. We've removed all the tubes and everything. You can go be with him, if you want. If you'd rather not, we have a private room you can use to be alone and make calls or whatever you need to do."

"Okay." Nat drew a breath that burned. "I'll stay with Dad. I need to call my . . . my friend."

"Sure thing." The nurse grasped Nat's shoulder. "You go on ahead. I'll get the paperwork together. Be thinking about what funeral home you want to come get him."

Funeral home? Christ, Nat hadn't ever even considered any such thing. How in the hell was he going to *do* this?

One step at a time, that's how.

Wiping his palms on his jeans, Nat started toward the room where he'd lived since Saturday. Every movement felt like a monumental effort. Like he was the Tin Man, rusted in place. He wondered if everyone else could hear his joints squealing when he walked.

Nat went to his father's bedside and peered down at him. He looked exactly like before, only . . . less. The absence of life left him gray and shrunken, still as a carving, mouth slack and eyelids half-open. When Nat touched his dad's face, he was relieved to find the skin still warm. He wasn't sure what he'd have done if his father had gone cold already.

He's dead. He's really dead. Gone forever.

Nat sank into the recliner, his mind whirling with everything that meant. Loss. Mourning. Bills. Paperwork. Memories. Telling Uncle Jeff and Abby, even if they didn't give a shit.

Freedom.

Guilt stabbed him. But the idea was there, and he couldn't unthink it.

Reaching through the side rail, he folded his fingers around his father's limp hand. "I'm sorry, Dad." He wasn't sure what exactly he was apologizing for. Not saving him? Not being the perfect son, maybe, whatever that meant?

No. Nat's father had never asked for salvation or perfection from his son. In his heart, Nat knew that *Sorry* was for all the resentments he'd let fester for so long, all the times he'd silently called his father a burden and wished to be rid of him.

Nat wasn't the superstitious type. He knew his private thoughts hadn't caused any of this. But that didn't make him feel any less awful for having thought them, or for being a tiny bit glad that this one responsibility, at least, was gone now.

He ran his thumb over his father's knuckles. Strange, how even the texture of his skin had changed with death. Like decay had been circling just out of sight, waiting for its chance to pounce, to rip away color and shape and warmth in its black beak and cruel claws.

Nat glanced up, as if he could spot his own personal demon vulture hovering over him, waiting for the life force to leave his human shell behind.

He dropped his father's hand—cooling, dissolving, *dead*—and stumbled across the room to press his forehead to the smooth glass of the window. It was still raining outside, an occasional bass rumble telling of a thunderstorm somewhere not far off. Soon, the nurse would come in with papers for him to sign, and strangers would take his father's body away. Back to Bluewater Bay, of course, because that was home, for both of them. And there would have to be a funeral, and people saying *I'm sorry* when they weren't, if anyone would even show up. Which was debatable.

And the bills . . .

Thinking about that right now was too overwhelming. It could wait a few days, anyway. Nat hoped.

Christ, he'd never felt so alone in his life.

You don't have to do any of this alone.

Nat's vision blurred. He blinked away the threatening tears. It felt like forever ago that Rafael had told him that. But he knew it was true.

He pulled his phone out of his pocket and dialed Rafael's number.

It took Rafael a lot longer than it should have to get to the hospital after Nat had called him, on account of heavy traffic slowed down by the rain. He finally found a spot in the parking garage and jogged across the breezeway into the lobby where they were supposed to meet, an hour and change after leaving his apartment.

Nat wasn't there.

Frowning, he circled the space a couple of times, checking all the chairs, even walking into the men's room and calling Nat's name. Nothing.

Back in the lobby, Rafael was wondering if he ought to call Nat and check on him when he emerged from the elevator bay. He didn't seem to notice Rafael, or anything else, his focus turned inward and his eyes glazed.

"Nat. Hey." Rafael hurried forward, only touching Nat's arm when he finally blinked and turned toward him. "Are you okay?"

Nat started to say something, then stopped and shook his head. "I don't know. I'm just so tired."

In fact, he looked worn out, still in the same clothes he'd been wearing two days ago, blue circles under his eyes, hair greasy and tangled. Soft golden whiskers covered his jaw and straggled down his throat.

Rafael hurt for him. "Are you ready to go?"

"Yeah." Nat peered at him with dull, exhausted eyes. "It's too much, Rafael. I can't think about it all yet."

Rafael wasn't sure what exactly he meant, but it didn't matter. Deciding he didn't care what anyone else in the lobby thought, he slipped an arm around Nat's waist and led him toward the exit. "You don't have to think about anything right now. I'm taking you back to my place, you're going to have a shower and something to eat, then you're going to sleep as long as you need to. We'll sit down together and think about things after that. All right?"

Nat said nothing, but his taut muscles relaxed under Rafael's arm. That was answer enough.

The rain and the traffic both slacked off as they left Port Angeles. Thick clouds still covered the sky, thankfully shielding Rafael from the setting sun as he drove west. Nat stared out the window the whole time without speaking. Rafael didn't break the silence. If Nat didn't want to talk, Rafael wasn't going to push him.

By the time Rafael pulled into his apartment complex, the remaining drizzle had stopped altogether, and a few rays from the fast-sinking sun peeked underneath the ragged edges of the clouds.

Ever since his first day in Bluewater Bay, Rafael had found the sunset spectacularly beautiful. Even here, in the parking lot of an unremarkable apartment complex with not the slightest glimpse of the Juan de Fuca Strait that had inspired the town's name, sunset—and sunrise, when he was up to see it—painted the place with magic. He always stopped what he was doing to admire it, if only for a second or two.

He'd caught Nat doing the same more than once. But today, he shuffled on, head down, ignoring the way the level shafts of light washed the world in red and orange.

Rafael decided to take the elevator today instead of the stairs. Nat didn't argue, which said a lot about both his physical and mental state. They got upstairs and down the hall to Rafael's apartment without running into any neighbors, for which Rafael was grateful. He didn't want to stop to talk with anyone, and he figured Nat wouldn't either.

Inside his apartment, Rafael finally gave in to the gnawing desire to wrap Nat in his arms. Nat immediately relaxed into his embrace, head tucked into the curve of his shoulder and arms looped around his waist. He breathed a long sigh into Rafael's neck. "I remembered what you said. About how I don't have to do this alone. That . . ." His voice caught. He pressed closer, clutching Rafael's shirt in both fists. "That's everything to me. Okay? *Everything.*"

Rafael's throat went tight. He stroked Nat's tangled hair. Rubbed circles between his shoulder blades. "I'm always here for you." He'd said it before, and would say it again, as many times as Nat needed to hear it.

"I know." Nat lifted his head. His expression was raw, wounded, all his walls beaten to dust. "I love you."

The fist around Rafael's ribs constricted, stealing his breath. He laid a palm on Nat's stubbly cheek. "And I love you."

Nat's smile was an anemic shadow of his usual devilish grin, but right then it was the most beautiful thing in the universe. "Romance is alive and well. We're the goddamn proof."

Rafael let out a startled laugh. "It's not official until I kiss you, though." He tilted his head and kissed Nat's too-pale lips. "There. Now we're a certified romance novel couple."

"Yeah." Nat snickered, then stopped, looking horrified. "Fuck. I shouldn't laugh."

Christ. Poor Nat. Raphael kissed him again, soft and lingering, comforting rather than sexual. "It's okay. It proves you're alive. That's all."

"Alive. Right." Nat stared at him, white-blue eyes wide and haunted. "What do I do now?"

Rafael didn't think he was talking about right now, tonight. He rested his forehead against Nat's. "We'll figure it out, together. I promise. Right now, let's get you cleaned up and fed, then you need to sleep."

"Yeah." Nat nodded. Sighed. He sagged a little in Rafael's arms. "You'll stay with me, right?"

And there went the hard, tight heat again, ballooning in Rafael's chest until it pushed his organs aside and filled his rib cage with light. He wound his fingers into Nat's hair. "Of course I will. I won't leave you. Not ever."

To him, that vow extended well beyond these walls, or this night. He thought Nat knew that too.

CHAPTER FOURTEEN

The day of the funeral was as sunny and bright as the day of Nat's father's death had been dreary and rainy. Nat wasn't sure what to think of that, except he was glad he didn't have to stand in the cemetery in the rain. That would have been *way* too much like some overwrought movie.

At least he had Rafael to help him handle the details. Sure, Cooper & Prince Funeral Home was super helpful—which was a good thing, since they were the only game in town—but still, Nat didn't think he'd have been able to face a single decision without Rafael to guide him.

As it was, every step of the process had felt like yanking an abscessed tooth without Novocain: horrifically painful, but a relief once it was over.

Now, standing in the slightly overgrown green grass and listening to the preacher talk about shit he couldn't believe, but his father had paid occasional lip service to, Nat felt like he was standing on the edge of a cliff. Before him lay the yawning gulf of the unknown future, terrifying and exhilarating. And here he was, unable to fucking jump because his feet were still tangled in the past. The whole business made him want to scream. At himself, at his dead father, at the world in general.

Rafael nudged him in time for the prayer. Nat bowed his head along with everyone else when the pastor—what was his name, anyhow?—glared at him, but he didn't close his eyes. He was the fucking bereaved here, he'd skip the fucking prayer if he wanted.

And, yeah, he was the *only* bereaved, because his sister hadn't flown out for the funeral. Big shock. She'd called him after he'd texted her the news of their dad's death, which *had* been kind of a surprise, and they'd talked for almost an hour. *"I'm proud of you,"* she'd said, which he'd never expected to hear from any of his dwindling family in his lifetime. *"Me and Colin watch* Wolf's Landing *every week. I tell everyone you're my brother. You've got a hell of a talent. Don't forget that, and don't waste it."*

Nice as that was to hear, having her at his side right now, when their father's casket was being lowered into the ground, would've been better. But apparently expecting his fucking *sister* to fucking *be there* for him for a change was asking too damn much.

"Amen," said the preacher. He lifted his head and gave the crowd the sort of plastic smile preachers used at funerals when they didn't know either the dead person or any of the mourners. "Brothers and sisters, go in peace."

Nat let out a long breath and clutched Rafael's hand tight. He wasn't sure how to feel right now. His father was in the ground, and he was the only person in his family who'd bothered to show up. At least his sister had acknowledged that their dad's death was hard for him. Uncle Jeff had said, *"Good riddance,"* when Nat had called him, then not only hadn't come to the funeral, but hadn't even sent a fucking card.

"He's clearly a piece of shit," Rafael had said. Nat's shredded emotions tended to agree, even though he knew better, really. Jerome Horn hadn't ever been an easy person to like, though Nat had loved him in spite of everything. No, he hadn't been a perfect man. But who was? Not Nat. It hurt soul-deep that his family couldn't even be bothered to show up to the funeral for *his* sake.

"Nat?"

Startled, he looked up from his less-than-comfortable perch in a metal folding chair. Solari stood there, lovely as ever in a simple black dress, her hair up in a twist and her eyes red-rimmed as if she'd been crying.

Crying. For *him.*

Profoundly moved—not only that Solari had shown up and *cried* for him, but that so *many* of the *Wolf's Landing* cast and crew had come—Nat stood and hugged her tight. "Thank you for coming, Solari. That means a lot to me."

"Of course I came, dear. You're my friend." She drew back and took both his hands in hers, surprising him as always with her strong grip. "I'm so sorry, Nat. I lost my father when I was fourteen. I know how difficult it is. You have Rafael, and I'm so glad for that, but please know you can call me anytime you want to talk. All right?"

The tears that had so far refused to fall stung the backs of Nat's eyes. "Thank you." There was so much more he wanted to say, but it wouldn't come out. Instead, he pulled her close again. Kissed the top of her head, and hoped none of the media vultures were hanging around snapping pics. "Thank you."

She moved on with a watery smile to hug Rafael. Next came Anna, offering him more hugs and telling him she'd do everything she could to make the shooting schedule easy on him. Then Suz, red-eyed and sniffling, telling him she'd help him with fixing up his house, even selling it if that's what he wanted, and that her brother was a real estate agent and he'd already said he'd do it for free. Also whispering in his ear that she was glad he'd hooked up with Rafael, and she expected details. That made him laugh for the first time in what felt like forever. He hugged her hard, kissed her cheek, and promised her they'd get together for coffee soon.

After that came a parade of *Wolf's Landing* cast and crew, including Levi Pritchard and Carter Samuels. Nat had done scenes with both men, but he couldn't call either of them friends. Yet both had come to his father's funeral, when his own sister hadn't.

In a way, it made him feel better. The support of his coworkers gave him a level of strength he'd never experienced before, and hadn't expected.

In another way? It made his family's absence hurt even more. Which turned his anger from a controlled burn to a conflagration that threatened to destroy him from the inside out.

"I don't want to go back yet," he said when Rafael tried to lead him to the car. Rafael's car, because Nat hadn't wanted a limo. He had to turn away from Rafael's confused, worried face, and look at the hills instead. At the woods, where he could get away from all these people he liked and their well-meaning concern, and try to get a handle on the rage boiling over inside him before he exploded. "I'm sorry. I don't mean to be a pain. But I really need to be alone for a while." He cast a quick glance over his shoulder. "Is that okay?"

"Of course," Rafael said, because he was more perfect than anyone had a right to be. He grasped Nat's shoulders and pressed a gentle kiss to his cheek. "You have your phone, right? You'll call if you need me?"

"Yeah." Nat turned, wound his arms around Rafael's neck, and captured his mouth in a lingering kiss that hopefully said everything his words couldn't. How in the hell had someone like him been lucky enough to snag a person as great as Rafael? "I'm going for a walk in the woods. Wait for me at Hobb's Park. I'll be there soon."

"Okay." Rafael's forehead furrowed, his gaze turning intense. He sucked his lower lip into his mouth for a second, then let it go, touched Nat's cheek, and stepped back. "Be careful."

"Always." Nat managed a smile for his man, then spun and strode for the shelter of the forest.

Rafael knew that sneaking after Nat was wrong. That he would likely see it as a betrayal of his trust. But no matter how hard he tried to hide it—and he was clearly trying, with everything he had—Nat was barely holding himself together.

He could yell and be mad all he wanted later. Right now, Rafael wasn't about to let him wander around in the woods by himself. Not as long as he was walking an emotional knife-edge. If Nat ended up hurting himself, Rafael wouldn't be able to live with it.

Of course, deciding to follow Nat and actually doing it were two different things. Unlike Rafael, Nat was sure-footed on the narrow, winding trails he'd been hiking all his life, and his long stride ate up the distance so quickly Rafael barely kept him in sight. Within a few minutes, Rafael's goal had switched from simply keeping an eye on Nat to preventing himself from getting hopelessly lost.

He'd made up his mind to announce his presence before he lost track of Nat altogether, when Nat pushed through a particularly thick patch of undergrowth into a small clearing and stopped. Rafael drew closer as quietly as he could, keeping to the shadows. Instinct told him that Nat needed to be alone. However, since Rafael had no clue where he was and couldn't leave without Nat, he waited and watched, feeling like an interloper.

Because you are, idiot. God, he was stupid. When was he going to learn to mind his business and trust the people he loved instead of butting in?

Too late now.

Nervous and almost sick with regret, Rafael gnawed his thumbnail and watched. For several seconds, Nat stood there, as still as the trees, shoulders tense and fists clenched. Then, without warning, he threw his head back and screamed.

Badly startled, Rafael clamped both hands over his mouth to keep from shouting. He stared, heart in his mouth, while Nat screamed again, and again, and again, as fast as he could draw breath. He snatched up a fallen stick as long as his arm, whirled around, and bashed it against the nearest tree until it dissolved in a shower of splinters. His eyes glittered with rage and pain.

Rafael watched from behind an evergreen, his pulse pounding with an uncomfortable blend of pity, fear, and undeniable awe. This was what Nat had been holding inside since his father's death. Probably much longer. Rafael ached for him. For all the things he'd felt he had to hide all this time. Was *still* hiding, in fact. He'd tried to get away from everyone, even the man who loved him, so he could feel safe letting everything out.

And then you followed him like a total asshole. Good job.

Shit. Rafael glanced behind him, wondering if he could find his way back after all. But, no, he knew he couldn't. He'd get hopelessly lost, which wouldn't help either of them. No, he was going to have to face the music.

A horrible, feral growl from Nat tore a soft sound from Rafael's throat. He covered his mouth again, but Nat didn't seem to hear. He found another stick—more of a branch, really, at least three feet long and thicker than his arm—and started beating it to death against the ground, punctuating each blow with a shout. Dirt, grass, and pieces of wood flew each time he whacked the branch into the ground.

Rafael had never seen Nat out of control like this. It was terrifying. For the first time ever, Rafael was scared to approach Nat. Scared of being physically hurt. Not on purpose—Nat would never do that—but by accident.

When Nat pummeled his branch to splinters and started ripping briars out of the ground, still yelling—though his voice was starting to go—Rafael swallowed his fear and stepped to the edge of the clearing. "Nat? You okay?"

Nat stilled so fast Rafael got chills. *He's not actually a real werewolf, right?* He licked his lips and tried again. "Um. Nat? It's me. Rafael."

Nat turned toward Rafael. His cheeks were red from exertion, his chest heaving. Sweat plastered his hair to his face. "What're you doing here? I told you I'd meet you at Hobb's Park." His voice was hoarse from screaming.

"I know, but . . ." Rafael cleared his throat. Made himself move closer, in spite of the fury rolling off Nat in waves. "I was worried about you. I know I shouldn't have followed you. I'm really sorry. I wanted to make sure you were all right, that's all."

"I wanted to be alone. Now I'm not." Nat gestured at Rafael with one hand. Bleeding scratches scored his palm. He didn't seem to notice. "I don't need you to babysit me."

Shame settled like a stone in Rafael's gut. "I know you don't. And I know—I *know*—I overstepped, okay? I'm an idiot. I know that. I needed to make sure you were all right for my own peace of mind, but it was a dumbass thing to do. And I would've left, but I didn't know where I was and I knew I'd get lost if I tried to find my way back by myself, so. Yeah. I'm sorry." He closed the distance between them, took Nat's wrist, and inspected the cuts on his hand. "You're hurt."

Nat yanked his hand back. "I'm fine."

"You're obviously not. And I'm not just talking about the scratches."

"I wanted to come out here and let off some steam."

"I know." Rafael bit his lip and decided to say what he'd only now realized was actually bothering him. "Whatever's making you want to scream and hit things, you can tell me. You know? You can talk to me. I know you wanted to be alone. But you don't *have* to be."

Nat barked a short, sharp laugh. He rubbed his hand on his cheek, leaving a smear of blood. "I killed my dad, Hollywood. Fix *that* shit."

Of all the things Rafael had expected to hear, that wasn't one of them. Shaking his head, he framed Nat's face in his hands. "No. No, you didn't. What happened to your father was an accident, Nat. A terrible accident."

"But he called me." Nat closed his fingers over Rafael's wrists. He stared through Rafael, his pale eyes haunted. "If I'd answered the phone when he called, I could've saved him. I should've saved him."

So this was the agony tearing Nat apart from the inside. Rafael's heart broke. He caressed the corners of Nat's mouth with his thumbs. "It wouldn't have made any difference. I'm sure it wouldn't have. Please don't blame yourself. Your dad wouldn't have. He loved you."

Nat broke out of his grip so fast Rafael staggered backward. "You don't know anything about it!" Nat shouted. "He fucking well *would* blame me, and he'd be right. He was an addict. It was my job to take care of him, and I *failed*." Nat leaned close, his face contorted. "Do you get that? I. Fucking. *Failed*!"

"Nat . . ." Rafael searched for something useful to say. Something to convince Nat that he wasn't to blame. But how did you change someone's mind when they'd made it up? "You can't keep blaming yourself. There was nothing else you could've done. You—"

"Shut up!"

Nat's echoing shout cut off Rafael's rambling speech so fast he bit his tongue. He stood there, shaking inside, watching helplessly while Nat stumbled back into the clearing, his palms pressed to his temples as if his head hurt.

"I couldn't help him." Nat breathed in, then let out a harsh sob. "I tried so hard, Rafael, I tried so fucking *hard*, but it wasn't enough. It was never enough, I couldn't do it. I couldn't save him. And he's dead." He took a step toward the trees. His knees buckled, and he collapsed in a heap on the ground. "Oh fuck, Rafael, my dad's *dead*, and it's my fault, but I keep on thinking about how I'm free of him now, and, fuck, I'm a terrible person." He curled up, knees to his chest and hands locked around the back of his neck.

When Nat's face crumpled and the tears started falling, all Rafael's fear and uncertainty dissolved like sugar in the rain. He hurried to Nat's side, knelt beside him, and gathered him close. "I'm here, baby. I'm here." He kissed the top of his head, clutched his shoulders tight. Made sure Nat felt the solid warmth of Rafael's body beside him. "Whatever you need, okay? Whatever you need, I'm here. I love you. And you're definitely *not* a terrible person."

A hard shudder ran through Nat's body. He lifted a hand, grasped Rafael's shirt, and clung. Deep, rough sobs shook Nat's body, his sorrow as out of control as his rage had been only a few minutes earlier. Rafael held him and stroked his damp hair while he finally let go of the grief and guilt he'd been keeping inside.

In Nat's dream, he ran through the trees, dodging thick trunks and wiry, grabbing brambles. Shadowy figures dashed ahead of him, at the edge of sight. His sister. His father, trailing darkness like streamers of death. And something else, something big and hulking that he wanted to catch more than he wanted to breathe. But the harder he ran, the farther he fell behind. Briars clutched at his ankles, stopping him. Anchoring him to the ground.

Wait, he called, silently, reaching for his family, for the looming bulk of his pie-in-the-sky dreams. The briars tightened, dragging him down into cold and darkness. Black earth filled his mouth and covered his eyes . . .

He woke to dim, filtered light and the taste of dirt on his tongue. Blinking, he concentrated on cataloging his surroundings—plain white walls, soft surface beneath him, neat wooden dresser a few feet away—until the dream let go and he remembered where he was, and why.

Raphael's apartment. Raphael's bed. The knowledge made him feel safe.

Moving carefully so he wouldn't wake Rafael, he pushed the sheet off and sat on the edge of the bed. Dull pain thumped through his skull for a second until his body adjusted to the position change. His whole head felt swollen, his eyes hot and his mouth cottony from breathing through it for the past who-knew-how-many hours, since his nose was stuffed up.

Crying hangover. Ugh.

The hurt punched him in the heart again. He fought the urge to double over with the force of it. How long was this going to happen? How long until he could remember his father was dead—*finally; no, stop thinking that, what's wrong with you?*—without wanting to curl up in a corner and hide?

At least he didn't feel like screaming and breaking things anymore. He never wanted to feel that level of uncontrolled anger again. He'd scared himself yesterday. Worse, he knew he'd scared Rafael too.

Rafael, who'd come after him in spite of his promise. Because he loved him. Which, yeah, had made Nat angry, especially at first. But at the same time, something cold and hard inside him had let go when Rafael had emerged from the trees and proved he wasn't alone.

Throat tight and aching, Nat rose and skirted the foot of the bed to stand peering down at Rafael. His round face looked even younger and sweeter in sleep. Like an innocent kid in need of protection. But Nat knew better. He'd experienced Rafael's inner strength firsthand. Rafael could handle anything life threw at him, and come out on top.

And he's mine.

Nat didn't know how he'd gotten so lucky, but he was glad of it.

Rafael stirred. Yawned. "Nat?" he mumbled, eyes still shut.

"Here." Nat sat on the edge of the mattress, leaned over, and kissed Rafael's lips. "Sorry, I didn't mean to wake you up."

"You didn't." Rafael pressed a palm to Nat's cheek. "Did you sleep okay?"

"Yeah." Better than he had in months, actually, in spite of the weird dream that had woken him.

"Good." Rafael raked his fingers through Nat's hair, watching him with those deep brown eyes that saw everything. "Are you all right?"

God, there were so many different answers to that question. Nat wasn't sure which one was right. "I think so, yeah," he said after a moment's thought. "Better than yesterday, anyhow. Which is a step in the right direction."

Rafael smiled. "Definitely." He pushed himself up to a sitting position and looped his arms around Nat's neck. "I know you'll need to deal with your dad's stuff at some point. But we'll do that when you're ready, not before. And we can either stay here, or at your place, whichever you'd rather do. Okay?"

An answering smile tugged at Nat's lips. "'We'?"

"Yeah, we." Determination hardened the soft curves of Rafael's face. "We're a team now, Wolfman. I'm not letting you go through any of this alone. And, okay, if you really *want* to live by yourself, I won't force myself on you, 'cause that would be creepy. But I'd really like it if we could live together."

A light, happy warmth blossomed in Nat's chest. "I'd like that too. And honestly, I don't think my place is even livable right now, with the fire damage and all, even if I wanted to go back there. Which I kind of don't."

"Then you'll stay here with me. And when you're ready to clean out your father's things, we'll go do it together."

Nat nodded, not trusting himself to answer. Rafael pulled him close for a kiss, and Nat melted into it. He'd never pictured himself falling for anyone, really, but especially not for such a genuinely nice person. And Rafael *was* nice. Kind, generous, and caring. He reminded Nat of his mother. How she'd always smiled and laughed, no matter what. How she'd always tried to play with him, even when she was sick. Even during the final days of the bone cancer that had etched what he now knew were permanent pain lines into her beautiful face, and finally killed her in spite of how hard she'd fought it.

"My dad would've liked you." Nat stroked Rafael's cheek. "I wish I'd introduced you. I never even gave him a chance to know you and accept us being together. And now it's too late."

"I would've loved getting to know him." Rafael pressed tiny kisses to Nat's nose, his chin, his cheek. "But you can't see the future, Nat. No one can. Don't blame yourself. Just believe that he would've wanted you to be happy. You loved him, and I can't believe you'd love someone who was completely unworthy of it. Not even your father."

Nat blinked. "I never thought of it like that."

"Yeah, well. Sometimes we all need someone else to point out stuff we can't see about ourselves." Rafael took both Nat's hands in his, lacing their fingers together. "I never met your father. But I have to believe he loved you, and wanted you to be happy. You need to believe that too."

God, he's right.

The grief that had lived in Nat's skin ever since this nightmare had begun welled inside him. But for the first time, it no longer felt like a ravening monster trying to claw him apart. It had been calmed. Tamed. Thinking of his father's death would always hurt. But maybe one day, it would fade enough to let him think of the good without the bad and painful overwhelming it.

For the first time in a long, long while, Nat saw a bright future opening up before him. And he thought his dad would be happy for him.

CHAPTER FIFTEEN

"I think I'm ready now."

Rafael paused with the refrigerator door open. He'd been waiting to hear Nat say those words for three weeks. Was this too soon? Too late? Rafael had no clue. He'd never lost anyone so close to him before.

At least he hadn't pushed Nat one way or the other. After realizing how badly he'd screwed up after the funeral, Rafael had promised to let Nat decide what was best for himself without Rafael trying to impose his own version of "best." He was shocked and ashamed by how *hard* that was. Which made him glad he'd decided to try. It made him a better person, and he wanted to be a better person for Nat.

Grabbing the milk, he pulled it out and shut the door with his elbow. "Okay. We can go today, then. If you're sure." He went to the table, studying the thoughtful expression on Nat's face. "So. You're sure?"

Nat's lips quirked into his usual sharp smile. "Yeah, I'm sure. Suz's brother called me yesterday and said there was an offer on the house. Which means I need to get off my ass and get Dad's stuff sorted out."

"Oh. Okay." Rafael poured milk on his oatmeal, then handed the carton to Nat. "Cool that somebody wants to buy the house. What're they offering?"

"I didn't ask."

Shocked, Rafael gaped at Nat. "What? Don't you want to know—"

"Nope." Nat pinned him with a wolf-eyed glare that shut him up double quick. "Look, it's the one and only offer I've gotten so far. I'm not looking to make money. It's not like I owe anything on the house. Mom and Dad got it before Abby and me were even born. And let's face facts here: it's in bad shape, in a bad neighborhood. If there's anybody at all out there willing to take it off my hands, I'm damn lucky."

He was right. Still, Rafael wanted to argue, on general principle. "Whoever buys it will be a few doors down from Ari Valentine. You could probably get more money for that, if you marketed it that way."

Nat rolled his eyes. "Look, I like Ari. He's okay. But I'm not gonna try to dig for more profit because this place is close to his. His glorious presence hasn't exactly improved the neighborhood, you know."

Grinning, Rafael spooned brown sugar into his oatmeal. "Be careful. People might figure out that you're a nice guy."

"Heaven forbid." Nat arched one fair eyebrow as he sipped his coffee. He reached across the table, taking Rafael's free hand in his. "Thanks for being so patient with me. I know I haven't been easy to live with."

That was so far from true, Rafael almost laughed. He stifled it, since Nat might've misunderstood.

"Not even a little bit." Rafael squeezed Nat's fingers. "We're both off today, so we can take all the time you need."

Nat's throat worked. He went back to his breakfast with a nod and a swift, grateful smile. "How's Solari?"

Rafael sighed. She and Gina had broken up a few days ago. Official word was that the decision had been mutual, but Rafael knew Solari had been the one to break it off. Gina had kept quiet in public, though she'd sent Solari plenty of texts—first pleading, then angry—since Solari wouldn't answer her calls after the first one had erupted into name-calling. Publicly, Solari had met the challenge like the class act she was: her head held high and her smile bright as ever. She responded graciously to messages of support online, and ignored the inevitable insults and outright threats, telling fans and haters alike that she was fine, thanks very much. But privately, she was devastated, even though she'd initiated the split. As she'd said to Rafael, you didn't love someone for that long, through so many trials, and walk away from it without pain.

"She's holding up." Rafael spooned hot cereal into his mouth and swallowed. "But it's been pretty tough on her. I'm worried about her."

"Because you worry about everybody you love. That's how you roll." Nat gazed at him with a soft smile and shining eyes, thumb caressing the back of his hand. "She's got us for friends. We'll make sure she doesn't have to face this shit by herself."

"Absolutely." Rafael watched the heat flare in Nat's eyes for the first time in weeks, and felt an answering fire in his gut. "I'm gonna take a shower before we head out. Want to join me?"

The mischievous twist of Nat's lips pulled at Rafael's heart like a hook. "You bet your sweet ass, Hollywood."

A couple of hours later, Nat stood on the sagging front steps of the house where he'd grown up, clutching Rafael's hand hard and trying to talk his feet into walking that last little distance to the door.

It was a lot harder than he'd figured on.

Rafael moved in front of him, partially blocking his view of the shabby old place. "You don't have to, Nat. There's no rush."

Nat studied Rafael's sweet, serious, concerned face, and fell a little bit more in love with him. "There is, though. The more I think about it, the more I realize I want this house out of my life. I want it sold so I can move on. The fire damage is as fixed as I can afford, and there's a solid offer on the table. I need to clear out Dad's stuff. And mine, for that matter; most of my junk's still here. It's about time I ripped off the Band-Aid and did it already."

"Yeah, I see your point. But I don't want you to feel like you're being pushed into something you're not really ready for."

"I know. But I'm not being pushed. I'm as ready as I'm ever gonna be." Smiling, Nat trailed his fingertips over Rafael's cheek and down over the faint marks on his throat, evidence of that morning's shower romp. "Besides, if I get sad, you can comfort me. With your dick."

Rafael let out a startled laugh. "Hey, whatever makes you happy."

"Your dick makes me pretty happy." Rafael laughed again, cheeks flushing deep pink, and Nat had to pull him close for a kiss. "*You* make me happy. That's why I can do this. Any of it. 'Cause of you."

Rafael's lips curved against Nat's. "You're selling yourself short. But thank you anyway."

A door squeaked across the street. Nat drew back reluctantly. Some of his neighbors were okay, but others could get nasty in their bigotry. He didn't want to find out the hard way which one was stepping outside right now.

Time to stop avoiding the job, Wolfman. Squaring his shoulders, Nat pulled his keys out of his pocket, climbed the front steps, and opened the door.

Between the two of them, they got everything cleared out in about five hours. Nat was surprised. He could've sworn he and his dad had more stuff than that.

Rafael duct-taped a box of clothes shut and set it next to the others beside the front door. "Okay. That's the last one, I think."

"Yeah. I already put all the stuff I'm actually keeping in your trunk. It's not that much." Nat planted both hands on the small of his back and stretched. "I guess we'll load all this into my truck and I'll take it to the shelter or something."

"Good idea." Rafael patted the back of the ancient sofa. "What d'you want to do with this furniture?"

"Leave it. The new owners can keep it, sell it, or dump it. I don't care."

Rafael's eyebrows went up. "Really?"

"Yeah, really."

The truth of that surprised Nat, but he meant it. With his father gone, he found that neither the house nor anything in it held any sentimental value for him. He'd kept his own things and a few personal items of his dad's that reminded him of the old days, when his father had been well and whole, but that was it. Everything else was nothing but a burden, and he wanted the objects gone, along with the memories that clung to them.

They'd loaded all the stuff in Nat's truck and were making one final sweep through the house—to make sure Nat didn't leave behind anything he actually needed, or so he told himself—when Rafael let out a sharp gasp. "Oh my God."

Frowning, Nat turned to face Rafael, who was staring wide-eyed at his phone. "What's wrong?" A terrible thought struck him. He grasped Rafael's shoulders. "Shit, are your parents all right?" Rafael adored his family. If anything had happened to them . . .

"They're fine. It's not that." Rafael lifted his head, shock stamped all over his face. "We have an email from SpectreVision. They contacted us about *Inside*."

Nat gaped. He wasn't in the same class of movie buff as Rafael, but he wasn't entirely ignorant either. He'd heard of the indie production company behind one of the few vampire films—other than *Nosferatu*—that he'd ever had any use for. "What? Why? Are they backing us?" The Kickstarter for *Inside* had gathered a respectable number of backers during the time it had been up, but it wasn't fully funded yet, and Rafael had started to get nervous that they wouldn't make the goal. This could put them over the top in a big way.

"No."

Okay. "Well, then . . . ?" Nat circled both hands in the universal *get on with it already* gesture.

A wide smile spread over Rafael's face, like sunshine breaking through clouds. "They want *Inside*."

Nat blinked. "What? What do you mean, they *want* it?"

"I mean, they want to buy it, produce it. Make a movie of it."

"They . . . they want . . ." The idea started to sink in. Nat stared at Rafael. "Okay, well, then, would you and me . . ."

"Would I direct, and would you star?" Rafael nodded, dark eyes shining. "Yeah. They said they want to hire me as the director, and you as the lead actor. They said it's clear from the sample footage that the film needs us both."

"Oh." The world wobbled. Nat clung to Rafael for support. "Oh shit. This is really happening." He gripped Rafael's shoulders again. "It is, right? I mean, you *did* say yes, right?"

"Well, I haven't had a chance to answer yet, but c'mon, of course I'm saying yes."

For a second, they stood there, staring at each other in silence. Then Nat whooped, Rafael laughed, and they threw their arms around each other, jumping up and down in Nat's living room like a couple of kids.

In fact, Nat *felt* like a kid, his joy wild and unfettered in a way it hadn't been in longer than he could remember.

His grief hadn't gone away. It was waiting for him, lurking like an unwelcome guest, ready to grab him and drag him down when he wasn't looking. But that was okay. He had a good life now. A job he loved, a man he loved, a future to look forward to. He could mourn for his father—both the man he'd been, and all the lost opportunities he represented—without letting his grief drown him.

When he'd settled down enough, Rafael dug his fingers into their usual spot in Nat's hair and peered up at him with a strange, vulnerable expression. "Well. I guess since we've got ourselves a production company, we'd better get busy working out the details for our movie."

"Definitely." Nat tilted his head to kiss away the uncertainty in Rafael's eyes. "It's okay to be happy about this."

"Yeah, I mean, I know, but . . ." Rafael shrugged, embarrassment written all over him. "You just lost your dad. It feels weird to be so excited about this right now."

"It's not weird. This is awesome news. Of *course* you're excited. So am I." Nat gave Rafael's butt a double-handed grope, because he could. "After everything that's happened lately, I like having something to celebrate."

"Good. I'm glad." Rafael smiled, so bright it stole Nat's breath. "Hey, let's go out. You want to?"

"You buying?"

Rafael laughed. "Yep. You ready now, or do you need more time?"

"I'm ready."

With one more tug on Nat's hair, Rafael let him go and led the way outside. Nat paused on the threshold, studying the place that had been his home for so long, through good times and bad. Leaving this house felt like finishing a book you both hated and loved; one you'd wanted to throw at the wall a few times, but ultimately valued for its flaws as much as its beauties. Now, it was time to pass it into different hands and start a new one.

Smiling, Nat locked the door on his past and followed Rafael into their future.

Dear Reader,

Thank you for reading Ally Blue's *No Small Parts*!

We know your time is precious and you have many, many entertainment options, so it means a lot that you've chosen to spend your time reading. We really hope you enjoyed it.

We'd be honored if you'd consider posting a review—good or bad—on sites like **Amazon, Barnes & Noble, Kobo, Goodreads, Twitter, Facebook, Tumblr,** and your blog or website. We'd also be honored if you told your friends and family about this book. Word of mouth is a book's lifeblood!

For more information on upcoming releases, author interviews, blog tours, contests, giveaways, and more, please sign up for our weekly, spam-free newsletter and visit us around the web:

Newsletter: tinyurl.com/RiptideSignup
Twitter: twitter.com/RiptideBooks
Facebook: facebook.com/RiptidePublishing
Goodreads: tinyurl.com/RiptideOnGoodreads
Tumblr: riptidepublishing.tumblr.com

Thank you so much for Reading the Rainbow!

RiptidePublishing.com

The Secret of Hunter's Bog
Down
Long the Mile
Flesh and Song (in the *Bump in the Night* anthology)
Hell's End (Hellscape, #1)
Hell On Earth (Hellscape, #2)
Demon Dog (Mojo Mysteries, #1)
A Ghost Most Elusive (Mojo Mysteries, #2)
Oleander House (Bay City Paranormal Investigations, #1)
What Hides Inside (Bay City Paranormal Investigations, #2)
Twilight (Bay City Paranormal Investigations, #3)
Closer (Bay City Paranormal Investigations, #4)
An Inner Darkness (Bay City Paranormal Investigations, #5)
Where The Heart Is (a BCPI related story)
Love, Like Ghosts (a BCPI related story)
Love's Evolution (Love's Evolution, #1)
Life, Love, and Lemon Cookies (Love's Evolution, #2)
Dragon's Kiss (Mother Earth, #1)
Shenandoah (Mother Earth, #2)
Convergence (Mother Earth, #3)
Adder
All The Moon Long (in the *Shifting Sands* anthology)
Catching A Buzz (in the *Temperature's Rising* anthology)

For a complete booklist, please visit www.allyblue.com.

Ally Blue is acknowledged by the world at large (or at least by her heroes, who tend to suffer a lot) as the Popess of Gay Angst. She has a great big suggestively shaped hat and rides in a bullet-proof Plexiglas bubble in Christmas parades. Her harem of manwhores does double duty as bodyguards and inspirational entertainment. Her favorite band is Radiohead, her favorite color is lime green and her favorite way to waste a perfectly good Saturday is to watch all three extended-version LOTR movies in a row. Her ultimate dream is to one day ditch the evil day job and support the family on manlove alone. She is not a hippie or a brain surgeon, no matter what her kids' friends say.

Website: allyblue.com
FB profile: facebook.com/AllyBlue.author
FB fan page: facebook.com/pages/Ally-Blue/98548113963
Twitter: twitter.com/PopessAllyBlue
Pinterest: pinterest.com/popessallyblue
Tumblr: therealallyblue.tumblr.com
Goodreads: goodreads.com/author/show/34997.Ally_Blue
Newsletter: Blue's News: Ally Blue's newsletter

Enjoy more stories like
No Small Parts
at RiptidePublishing.com!

Clickbait
ISBN: 978-1-62649-495-4

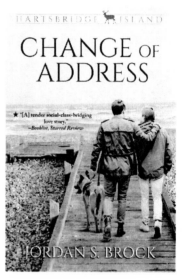

Change of Address
ISBN: 978-1-62649-464-0

Earn Bonus Bucks!
Earn 1 Bonus Buck for each dollar you spend. Find out how at
RiptidePublishing.com/news/bonus-bucks.

Win Free Ebooks for a Year!
Pre-order coming soon titles directly through our site and you'll
receive one entry into a drawing for a chance to win free books for
a year! Get the details at RiptidePublishing.com/contests.

CPSIA information can be obtained
at www.ICGtesting.com
Printed in the USA
LVOW11s2334150217
524373LV00003BA/722/P